"I may appear to be a good man, but I don't feel like one. What I am at the moment is a man who needs to remember who and what he really is."

"And what's that?"

"A rancher to the bone. This land has been in my family for generations. I love this place; I belong to this place. The fact that I'm…distracted right now doesn't change things. We both know that I'm the rancher and you're the model. And Lily is stuck dead in the middle because she's still so innocent that she could decide she likes you, latch on and get hurt when you go."

Ivy sucked in a deep breath. She felt as if she'd been kicked. "I would *never* put a child in a position where she could be hurt."

"I didn't mean it that way. See? I rush into things like a bull and say things that come out wrong. I'm a harsh man of the land and you're…not. Ivy…" He groaned. "You make me crazy. You have from the start. I didn't want to hire you."

"And now you regret it?"

"Yes. No. Yes. Come here." He slipped an arm around her waist and drew her to him. He rested his forehead against hers. Then, without warning, he tugged her closer. His mouth crushed hers.

Dear Reader

A runway model and a cowboy? How is that going to work? I thought, when Ivy Seacrest and Noah Ballenger walked into my imagination.

Ivy:

- Tall, thin and ethereal, almost fragile-looking. A strong Montana wind would surely blow her over.

- Her face has launched a thousand products.

- She knows about make-up and hair, and she likes cute little scarves and belts that don't belong anywhere near a ranch.

Noah:

- A man born to roam the land.

- He's big and rugged and not always careful about what he says.

- He knows about horses and hay and how to rope a steer, and he doesn't get into town too often…by choice.

These two are going to be trouble, I thought. *How am I ever going to get them to hook up or even get along for more than five minutes?*

Then things got worse. Ivy, I found out, couldn't look at Noah's child without having her heart rip in two. Noah couldn't stand the fact that anyone would shy away from his baby. What was more, Ivy, it seemed, had a sassy mouth on her, and Noah wasn't used to that! Really, these two gave me fits…right up until the day they stopped… and made my heart melt.

Welcome to the runway…and the ranch. It's going to get warm in here—in the best way possible. I hope you enjoy the show.

Best wishes

Myrna Mackenzie

COWGIRL
MAKES THREE

BY
MYRNA MACKENZIE

First published in Great Britain 2010
Harlequin Mills & Boon Limited,
Eton House, 18-24 Paradise Road, Richmond, Surrey TW9 1SR

© Myrna Topol 2010

ISBN: 978 0 263 21439 0

Har~~lequin Mills~~ ... ~~ural,
rene~~ ... own in
sust~~ ... conform
to t~~ ... in.

Prin~~ted and bound~~
by ~~...~~

Myrna Mackenzie grew up not having a clue what she wanted to be—she hadn't been born a princess, the one job she thought she might like because of the steady flow of pretty dresses and crowns—but she knew that she loved stories and happy endings, so falling into life as a romance writer was pretty much inevitable. An award-winning author, with over thirty-five novels written, Myrna was born in a small town in Dunklin County, Missouri, grew up just outside Chicago, and now divides her time between two lakes in Chicago and Wisconsin—both very different and both very beautiful. She adores the internet (which still seems magical after all these years), loves coffee, hiking, attempting gardening (without much success), cooking and knitting. Readers (and other potential gardeners, cooks, knitters, writers, etc.) can visit Myrna online at www.myrnamackenzie.com, or write to her at PO Box 225, La Grange, IL 60525, USA.

To the ladies of
The Daisy Morris Nutrition and Activity Center
in Campbell, Missouri, my home town.
This one's for you!

PROLOGUE

IVY SEACREST STRUGGLED to keep her chin high and her backbone straight. She forced herself to stare directly at Melanie Pressman. "Are you sure you don't have any openings at the diner? I'm not afraid of hard work."

Melanie's smile was small and condescending. "Afraid not. I'd like to do something for an old…friend, but I just don't have a thing."

Right. Ivy and Melanie had never been friends. They'd never been anything, even when Ivy had been living here in Tallula, Montana, ten years ago.

Given the situation, Ivy knew the smart thing to do was hold on to the few shreds of pride she still retained after these past few days of begging for a job and just walk away. Melanie wasn't going to help her any more than anyone else had. But her situation was desperate enough that Ivy had to try one more time. Looking around to see what menial position she could volunteer for, she opened her mouth.

The bell over the door jingled as Melanie's portly husband, Bob, entered the diner. He smiled. "Hey, Ivy. I heard you were back in town. You staying for a while?"

Ivy nodded even though she wasn't planning on staying any longer than she had to. She turned back to face Melanie, but even the small smile was missing from the woman's face now. Ivy could practically feel the cold blow-ing off the woman. It had been that way with almost every married woman in town. As if they thought she had come here expressly to lead their husbands down the path of sin.

"I could clean," she told Melanie, knowing that even that was futile now. Melanie had the look of a woman out to protect her territory.

"I told you no," Melanie said. "I don't have any jobs open at all. Nobody here in town does."

Which came as no surprise. This had been Ivy's last chance, and she wouldn't even have tried it, knowing how slim her odds were, if she hadn't needed the money so badly.

She turned to leave.

"Nobody in town, I guess," Bob said, "but I heard that Noah Ballenger was looking to hire a ranch hand."

Even though Ivy's back was turned, she heard Melanie's hiss behind her. "Ivy's a *fashion model*. Don't you know that? She doesn't hang out with ranchers and people like us anymore. She doesn't do ranch chores. Things have changed."

They certainly had, Ivy thought as she stalked toward the door. Her world had come tumbling down. She'd lost everything that mattered. The pain and the memories threatened to make her stumble, but somehow she stayed on her feet.

"I'll try that. Thank you, Bob," she managed to say.

"Stupid man. Noah's not going to hire her, and he's not going to thank you, Bob," Melanie said as Ivy left the diner.

Ivy knew that both of those statements were probably true.

Too bad I can't afford to care, she thought as she headed down the road that led to Noah Ballenger's ranch.

CHAPTER ONE

NOAH BALLENGER SQUEEZED the telephone receiver so hard it felt as if it might break in his hand. "What do you mean Ivy Seacrest is on her way over here to apply for a job as a ranch hand? Because you told her I was hiring? Well…untell her. You should know that I can't hire her. She doesn't belong here, and I don't have anything that a woman like her could actually do. I don't care that she was raised in Tallula. She was a princess when she lived here and she's been an international model for ten years. Whatever she wants, I don't have it here and I never will."

The answer came swiftly. It was too late to retract whatever had been said earlier. Ivy was already on her way, and no one in town knew how to reach her. Noah would have to be the bad guy and tell her no.

He frowned at the telephone and hung up. Ivy Seacrest? Not going to happen.

Noah had hardly known Ivy when she'd lived here. She'd been only eighteen when she'd left, four years younger than Noah. What little he did know from what he'd heard and the little he'd seen was that Ivy had possessed the type of rare beauty that had made people sit up and notice, and pretty much every man in town would have killed just to get her to smile at him. Noah had been the exception. He'd spent his younger years living, breathing and learning the ranch empire that had been in his family for generations and would one day be his, and when Ivy had been old enough for him to notice properly, he'd been away at college…falling in love with a woman who was totally wrong for a rancher. A woman who had nearly broken him in more ways than one. A woman not much different from Ivy.

Because of that experience, that woman, that completely misplaced and impossible obsession of his, other shaky dominoes had been put into play.

Old, nearly forgotten pain tinged with a sense of betrayal ricocheted through Noah, but he let it come. He needed to remember that because of his bad experience with Gillian, he had gone on to do things he regretted. Terribly. All because he was stupid enough to forget that Ballenger Ranch was his world, his destiny. It was his legacy to his baby daughter, and nothing and no one who didn't fit with that image belonged here.

Ivy Seacrest was an exotic interloper from some other world. She didn't belong in this town that had been built on cattle. He had no idea why she would even return to Tallula, since she hadn't come back when her father had died a year ago. He sure as hell had no idea why she would try to hire on as a ranch hand. Maybe it was a publicity stunt. Something to do with her modeling career.

He didn't know or care, but no way was he letting her on his ranch. He'd done his stint with beautiful, misplaced women. One of them had broken his heart. Another had betrayed him *and* his child, because she'd changed her mind about being a rancher's wife after the deed was already done.

He was through with all that. No more women.

"Turn your pretty butt around, Ivy," he muttered. "I don't like to be the bearer of bad news."

But he would do what he had to do. And what he had to do right now was send Ivy Seacrest packing.

Ivy stared at the long, low ranch house and nearly stumbled. She tried not to think about what she was about to do, what she had to do. Voluntarily spend time on a ranch, a world that she had sworn never to return to, a world filled with harsh and devastating memories. *No choice. Absolutely no choice,* she told herself. *Just do it. Grit your teeth and do it.*

Easy to say, but first she had to get Noah Ballenger to hire her, and she was pretty sure it wasn't going to be easy. Heck, it might be impossible.

No, I won't let it be impossible. I'm not letting him stop me, just because he doesn't like me.

She wasn't just kidding herself about Noah not liking her, either. When she had lived here ten years ago, Noah had been the only man who hadn't liked her. Or who hadn't appeared to notice her…which, back then, was pretty much the same thing.

Lots of girls had disliked her. That much was evident by how many times in the past few days she'd been turned down for jobs by those girls turned women.

But she had to have work, and ranching, much as she loathed it, even though it brought back awful, tragic memories, was the one thing other than modeling that she knew how to do. With modeling no longer an option, it was the *only* thing she knew how to do.

A wave of panic hit her, thinking about being back on a ranch. Living the life that had trapped her and obsessed her father so much that nothing else had ever mattered…

including the health of his wife and the well-being of his child.

Barraged by bad memories, Ivy still kept walking. Sometimes you had to go through fire to break free, and this job on this ranch was her ticket out of this town that had killed her mother and had nearly killed her own spirit. Noah Ballenger was her only hope.

Ivy started walking faster. *Get this over with. Get it done. Keep working until you've got enough money and then run away again as quickly as you can.*

She nearly sprinted to the door. There she took long, deep breaths. As ticked off as Melanie had been, she had probably called Noah to warn him that Ivy was headed his way, so with a little luck Noah would be at the house.

Still, Ivy hesitated. After hurrying to the door, she was suddenly hit with a wave of pure fear. Growing up on her father's ranch, she'd felt trapped, beaten down, with her whole identity ripped away from her. Now she was volunteering to step back into that kind of life. Was she insane?

No, I'm desperate. Just knock on the door, say whatever you have to say to get a job. This is only temporary. It won't be like the last time.

She was on the verge of almost being prepared mentally when the door swung open wide, and the entrance was blocked by a large, broad-shouldered man. Ivy surprised herself by having to look up. A tall woman, she was used to being at eye level with most men. Noah Ballenger was obviously taller than most men.

He was, she noted, like a wall. Big, imposing, dark haired and, from the forbidding look in his amber eyes, not happy to see her.

She wanted to close her eyes and run back to New York. Instead, she forced herself to stay rooted to the spot. She swallowed and tried to control her racing heartbeat and her breathing. "Hello," she managed to say, holding out her hand. "You probably don't remember me, Mr. Ballenger. My name's Ivy Seacrest. I used to live on the Seacrest Shores Ranch. I understand that you're hiring a ranch hand, and I'm here to apply for the job."

Ivy tried a professional-looking smile. It should have been easy. Her smile had once been her fortune. She'd been able to turn it on and off at will. But Noah was looking at her as if she was something…unpleasant. She just couldn't manage to make that smile work.

"I remember your family. I know who you are," he said without a trace of warmth in his voice.

She wondered what he remembered. There was plenty to remember, most of it bad.

"Bob Pressman told me that you were looking for a hired hand. I'd like to apply."

He gazed down at her with eyes that had been known to cause women in the town to melt. Ivy had heard the stories, heard the audible sighs, but right now she didn't have the luxury of melting, even though she felt trapped and overwhelmed by his gaze, her heart thundering. What she had was the distinct feeling that Noah was going to try to brush her off quickly.

"Maybe we could discuss this in your office," she suggested, holding out her hand and taking a small step forward in the hope that he would simply step aside and let her cross the threshold.

Bad idea. He moved, but forward, blocking her and bringing her outstretched fingertips into contact with his chest.

He looked down at her hand, not budging. She could feel the warmth of his skin seeping through the white cotton of his shirt, and her breathing kicked up a notch. There was something very virile about this man, something a bit wild lurking beneath the surface.

Noah Ballenger would be a hard man to handle. That was bad. Ivy was used to handling most men, and the ones she hadn't been able to had almost destroyed her.

She jerked her hand away. "Excuse me. I'm sorry. I—"

"Why?" he asked. "Why would you even want a job here? The word is that you hated ranching. You took off as soon as your looks won you a modeling contract. Don't try to tell me that you've rediscovered a love of the land."

Ivy looked way up into those amber eyes again, trying not to wince at Noah's reference to her looks. Her appearance had been the one thing she'd been able to count on, but the scars she bore now were a painful and constant reminder of the day everything she valued had been torn from her.

To her surprise, Noah was no longer frowning. His expression suggested a genuine need to know why she was here. But he still hadn't budged or suggested that he might grant her an interview.

She didn't want to have to explain herself.

But it didn't look as if she had a choice.

"Modeling isn't an option anymore." She had grown used to saying the words, so she could do it now without a trace of emotion in her voice, even though the frantic fear at having no way to make a living lurked right beneath the surface, threatening her composure.

He stared at her for a few seconds, the intensity of his expression making her feel naked, nervous. She had a terrible need to duck her head, look down, hide what he was seeing. Even worse, his scrutiny of her damaged face was threatening her composure. She had an awful inclination to go back, relive those devastating moments two years ago. *Don't, don't think about that day, please don't.* The words spilled out into her consciousness, saving her, and somehow she managed to keep staring directly at him. She forced herself not to remember the terrible, heartrending things that had brought her here to his door.

His nod was almost as brusque as hers had been. "If you say it's not an option, that's your choice, but that still doesn't explain your sudden interest in ranching when you hated it before."

Panic began to swirl within her. She didn't want to talk about her motives. "Does it matter? As long as I can do the job?"

"It depends," he said. "If I wasn't sure a man could do the job he claimed he could do, if his motives were suspect or if I would have to start the hiring process over in a few days because he decided that he'd changed his mind about working here, I'd ask a lot of questions."

She stood there, staring into those eyes. He didn't back down. Finally she looked away.

"Fair enough," she said. "I'm here because the taxes are due on my parents'...that is, on *my* ranch and I don't have the money."

"And you want to keep the property."

She shook her head. Hard. No, she hated that ranch. Just being there these past few days had brought back bitter memories. "I want to sell the ranch, but I have to pay the taxes before I can do that." Did the desperation show in her voice? Did she have any pride left at all?

Not much. She'd lost her pride along with her son, her husband and her career in a car crash two years ago, but she wasn't sharing any of that with this man.

"I'm sorry, but I don't want to talk about this. You have the right to ask me why I want the job. The answer is the same one many other people would give. I need work. I know ranching."

"You hate it. That fact still stands."

She wouldn't deny it. Ranching had ruled her father's world. It hadn't been good to her.

"I know how to do the work."

He looked doubtful. He looked as if she could tell him that she'd won the Ranch Hand of the Year award and it wouldn't have made a bit of difference to him.

"Why not take a job in town?"

Ivy took a deep breath. Should she tell him that she'd been turned away without an interview for every job the town had to offer? That snide smiles had accompanied the "Sorry, but no" responses she'd received?

No. Those were Noah's neighbors and friends.

"That's not an option, either," she said. And, in truth, those had been jobs that were outside her skill set anyway. This one wasn't.

He was slowly shaking his head. "You seem to have ruled out a lot of options, lady. But working here...it's just not possible."

"I'll work hard," she promised.

"I never said you wouldn't."

"So hire me. I heard that you needed someone."

"I need a big someone."

"I'm big."

For a minute she almost thought he was going to smile. He rubbed one hand over his jaw as if to hide his amusement. "You're tall. I need someone beefy."

"I'll eat more."

Now he did smile. Just a little. "Ivy..."

"I can do this, Noah."

He shook his head again. "I'm sorry, Ivy, but you'll find

something else. Something will open up in town. I need a man."

Now she visibly bristled. "That's discrimination. It's illegal."

"So sue me."

As if he knew that she wouldn't. She couldn't. There just wasn't time, even if she had the money for a lawyer. And if she had money, she would have already paid the taxes and left town.

"Aren't you even going to invite me in? Can't we talk about this? You could give me…I know…you could give me a test. Let me do some chores just to show you—"

"No," he said stopping her. "I'm sorry, Ivy. It's not happening. Goodbye."

With that, he stepped back and shut the door right in her face.

Ivy stood there for a few minutes. Anger, red and hot and simmering, bubbled inside her. Then she turned and walked away. And kept walking until she was out of sight of the house.

Forget it. It's over, she thought. What was she going to do?

She stopped and looked out over the land, at the barns and outbuildings, the machinery and fences. She could almost hear her father saying, "The land will never let you down." Maybe not, but it had stolen her life. His obsession with ranching had cost her a childhood, a father and her mother's life.

Still, standing there gazing at Noah's ranch, one much larger and more successful than her city-bred father's had been, she remembered helping pull a calf, feeding cattle in winter. She still knew how to do these things. And doing them would pay her way out of Tallula again. If she could just make it happen.

Turning toward the house again, she remembered Noah's last words. *It's not happening.*

"Maybe not, Noah," she whispered. "But it won't be for lack of trying. You haven't seen the last of me."

Noah stared out the window, watching Ivy's retreating back and feeling like the biggest jerk on earth. She walked away tall and proud, but he'd seen the stark disappointment in her eyes before she'd gone.

Not that that changed anything. He'd lived on this ranch all his life. It had been his since his father's death five years ago, and he had hired and fired a number of people during that time. Ballenger Ranch was what he would leave to his little girl when he was gone, and two-and-a-half-year-old Lily was the most important part of his world. He couldn't gamble with the ranch. He needed good, solid people working here.

Not someone who would hate the lifestyle and fly away at a moment's notice, leaving him in the lurch. He needed someone committed to ranching, and he knew all too well about people who weren't cut out for this life. He had a child with an absentee mother who was living proof of that.

It was his duty to protect his child from more cut-and-run people. So, much as he felt bad for Ivy's financial difficulties, much as he admired her for having the guts to ask him for this job again once he'd turned her down, he still couldn't deny that she didn't belong here.

While they'd been talking, he had been assessing. She was thin, almost fragile looking. Whether it was because of years of enforced model thinness or something else, he didn't know.

What he knew was that fragile didn't play well on a ranch.

"You could give me a test," she'd said, with those big blue-violet eyes practically snapping. Modeling wasn't an option anymore, she'd said. She'd reached up as if to touch her face, and he'd seen that her small nose bore a crease; her lips looked as if a part of them had been erased at one edge. He didn't know where she'd gotten those scars, but the scars didn't seem to matter to his body. Everything male in him had made him want to look closer.

And that, above all, let him know that she didn't belong here. She wasn't built for this life, and he couldn't survive mucking things up with a woman again. His soul just couldn't handle that kind of damage anymore. But more important than that, there was Lily to consider.

His daughter and the ranch were his world now. Forever. Both of them came before any needs or desires of his. Anyone who came here had to pass his Lily test. They couldn't negatively impact his world. So no, he couldn't allow himself to be swayed by a pair of pretty, blue-violet eyes or long legs or sun-kissed blond hair.

But he hoped that Ivy found some sort of work soon. He hoped she made enough money quickly. Then she'd be gone, and that would be a good thing, because he didn't trust himself to run into her in town and not appear interested.

That night after dinner he took Lily from Marta, his housekeeper babysitter, and went onto the porch to watch the sun going down. Brody, his foreman, was walking toward the house.

"I just got back from an errand in town. Word on the street is that Ivy Seacrest applied here today as a ranch hand," Brody said. The man's interest looked to be more than casual, and Noah remembered that Brody and Ivy were somewhere near the same age.

"Forget it, Brody. I'm not hiring Ivy so that you'll have

something prettier to look at than cows or the other hands. She's not coming back."

And Noah continued to think that right up until the moment he walked into his barn the next morning and found Ivy pitching hay into one of the horse stalls.

"Good morning, Noah," she said.

Ivy's hair was a color that defied description. Strands of honey were mixed with palest tan and pure blond, making a man want to look closer and let the strands slip between his fingertips. Her eyes were eager, her smile bright. Noah felt as if he'd been punched in the chest, so aware of the woman was he. He wasn't even going to allow himself to let his gaze drop to the way her pale blue shirt and denim jeans fit her curves. The fact that he was noticing any of this at all was bad news.

"Good morning, Ivy," he said. "Now, if I could just have my pitchfork back, I'll point you toward the door. I meant what I said yesterday."

Her smile froze. Her shoulders slumped just a trace before she caught herself.

"It was worth a try," she said. "I won't bother you anymore."

Too late, he thought. She was already bothering him. He was already thinking about her and worrying about her. It was a sickness, this fear that he would make another misstep with a woman.

Which didn't change a darned thing. "Not a problem," he said. "I admire your tenacity. I wish you luck."

She handed him the pitchfork, and even through the rough gloves she wore he was aware of her slender hands, those long fingers.

"You could have let her try," Brody said, coming up behind him once Ivy had gone.

With a swift turn of his body, Noah faced Brody. "I

did that once. I let Pamala try to play at being a rancher's wife. And where is she now? She's in California, playing at her new role of wannabe actress. She didn't even care enough about Lily to say goodbye. What am I going to tell my child when she wants to know why her mother never comes to see her? You think I want to expose her to more of that when Ivy is cut from the same cloth as Pamala was?"

Brody's face paled, but he didn't drop his gaze.

"You can't live your life letting your mistake with Pamala color everything you do."

Of course, Pamala had not been his first or only mistake with a woman, but that was none of Brody's business.

"Watch me," Noah said. "Ivy's not working here. I'll get the women in town to put some basic supplies together so that she's fed and clothed. But I am not giving her a job. And that's final."

No matter what she did or said, she was never going to be a part of Ballenger Ranch.

CHAPTER TWO

SHE HAD TOLD NOAH that she wouldn't bother him anymore, so why was she out here repairing a section of fence?

Ivy wrestled with her conscience. She acknowledged that simply trying to stay out of the man's way while still attempting to impress him with her ability to do the job was pushing the limits. But what could she do? She needed money to survive. If she could earn enough money to pay the taxes, she could sell the ranch. Then she could hide for a long time. No facing reporters wanting to ask her how losing Bo and Alden and her famous face had changed her life. It had been two years, but just as soon as she thought everyone had forgotten about her, some new model would shoot to the forefront and the reporters would seek her out again for a "whatever happened to" segment, and she just couldn't do that.

She'd enjoyed modeling and her looks had brought her honest work, but how she felt about the loss of those looks was…complicated. Her scars were a reminder of a life she had loved and lost, but even more than that, they were a reminder of her failure to save her baby, and she never hid them with makeup. She had lived while Bo died. She couldn't forgive herself for that, but she wouldn't discuss it, either. No. She needed anonymity and enough money to allow her to disappear.

So, yes, she felt guilty about her impulsive comment to Noah, but she couldn't give up. Taking her pliers in her gloved hand, she snipped the wire and pounded the staple home, snugging up the wire.

"Nice job, but it won't work, Ivy. Most of my fences are in good repair."

She whirled, and there he was. "How did you sneak up on me like that?"

"Applesauce knows how to be quiet." He patted the big black gelding.

"Applesauce? He looks more like a Thunder or Killer."

Noah almost smiled. "My daughter named him."

Daughter. Child. He had one. Hers was gone. The familiar arrow of pain bit deep, but she was ready. She'd heard that he had a child, so she was able to keep from crumbling. This time.

"She's a little young to be naming horses, isn't she?"

"Lily's almost three, but she loves horses and she also loves—"

"Applesauce," they said at the same time.

Ivy let that sink in. A man who would risk being ribbed by other men for riding a horse with a silly name in order to make a child happy seemed more human than she wanted to acknowledge.

"The horse is irrelevant, though," he said. "I'm not hiring you, Ivy. You're wasting your time and mine."

Okay, no matter that she was touched by his regard for his daughter, Noah was never going to be on her list of favorite men. If she had such a list, that is.

"You haven't even given me a chance."

"I don't have to. I own the ranch and I call the shots."

Desperation began to crawl through her bloodstream as she felt her last chance slipping away. "So you'll hire a man with inferior skills just so you won't have to hire a woman."

"I didn't say that."

"The fact that you won't even test my skills implies as much."

"Maybe I just don't want to hire an insubordinate employee."

"I wouldn't be insubordinate."

He chuckled. "Ivy, you're arguing with me. Isn't that the definition of being insubordinate?"

She frowned. "I know how to follow directions and be submissive." Unfortunately she knew that all too well. And the word *submissive*…maybe that hadn't been the best choice. He was looking at her as if she'd said something sexual. Then he swore.

"I'm sorry. You obviously have your reasons for pursuing this, but I have my reasons for saying no. It's not happening, Ivy."

She opened her mouth.

He groaned. "Give up, Ivy."

Something inside her cried out at the injustice, but she knew when she was beaten. She'd traveled this "no way to win" path before. In this very town. On the ranch she'd grown up on.

Pocketing her pliers, she turned to walk away.

"You don't have to walk. I'll arrange for you to ride."

She stopped, tipped her head back as she pivoted and stared up at him. "No. You have only one thing I want and that's all I'll accept from you." A ride was a pity gesture. She had what it took to do this job, even if Noah couldn't see it. Walking home was nothing. Deciding where she went with her life from here? That was the difficult part.

Still, she wouldn't let him see her fear. A frightened woman wouldn't change his mind. Ivy squared her shoulders and marched away. She and Noah were done, unless...

Stop it, she told herself. *There won't be any unless. He's made that clear.*

But then, she'd always had a stubborn, rebellious streak. Sometimes a good dose of stubborn was all a person had to see them through the day.

"What's that you're eating, pumpkin?" Noah asked his daughter.

Lily held out one chubby little hand, in which she clutched a mangled piece of toast with jam. She looked up at him with her huge blue eyes and smiled. "Cook-ie," she said with a little laugh.

Noah wiggled his eyebrows. "That looks like toast to me."

Lily giggled. "Cook-ie," she insisted.

"Marta, are you giving our girl cookies for breakfast?" he asked incredulously.

Marta gave a dramatic sigh. "She insisted."

Noah shook his head. He pointed to the toast. "No cookies for breakfast, Lily."

"Cookie," she said with another laugh, her blond curls swaying as her little body rocked with delight at this strange little routine she and her daddy had somehow fallen into.

Noah did his best to look stern. "Okay, hand over the cookie, Lilykins."

And here came the good part, the part she loved. "No. Toast," she said with great relish and popped a piece into her mouth.

"Ah, you are a clever one, sweetheart," he told her. "And

a stubborn one. You know how to get your way when you want to."

He was still thinking about that when he wandered outside to work. In her own way, Ivy reminded him of Lily. Stubborn and determined and proud and hard to resist.

Noah stopped in his tracks. That was a road he didn't want to travel. Ivy had no business invading his thoughts. That was how all bad things with women started—when you let ones you had nothing in common with start creeping into your thoughts uninvited. Next thing you knew you were in high water, unable to get back to shore or swim against the strength of the current, and they were leaving you. Or even worse, they were leaving Lily. Hurting her. Without so much as a drop of remorse.

Noah growled.

"Bad night?" Brody asked, coming up beside him in the barn.

"You sound hopeful."

Brody laughed. "Not at all, but if you did have a bad night, your day isn't going to be any better. Ed broke his leg last night and he's out of commission. Now we're down two hands instead of just one."

Noah's growl turned into a blue streak of cussing.

"Is that any way for a daddy to talk?"

"No, but Lily's inside, and I have good reason to swear. I recognize that look in your eyes."

"What look is that?"

"It's the 'I'm holding a good hand' look. You've wiped the floor with me at poker that way before, so let's not play games. Say what you've got to say."

"Okay, I will. The thing is…Ivy isn't just nice to look at. She's a determined worker. I saw her wade in and rescue a calf yesterday that had gotten caught in some muck."

"She did what? And you didn't tell me?"

"No point in telling you when you weren't listening."

"She was going. She wasn't coming back." But in Noah's mind he heard Lily holding a piece of toast and telling him that it was a cookie while she laughed at her own joke. Ivy might have left and intimated that she wasn't coming back, but she obviously had a stubborn streak as wide as his daughter's.

Now Brody was shaking his head. "She sure did a number on you, didn't she?"

Noah didn't ask who. Brody didn't know the half of what his wife had done or about the woman preceding her. And Noah had had enough. Without saying another word, he turned toward his car.

"If you're looking for Ivy, she's out at the corral getting acquainted with Bruiser."

Noah's heart lurched. "And you let her? I should have got rid of that horse long ago. I've been meaning to. Have to before Lily starts roaming around outside."

"I get the feeling Ivy isn't the kind of woman a man *lets* do anything. She has a mind of her own."

But Noah was through listening. Brody was clearly besotted and worthless where Ivy was concerned. Instead Noah made a beeline for the corral where Bruiser was penned alone. He had bought the horse one insane day a year ago when he'd finally realized that Pamala was never going to even make an attempt to be a mother. He'd been counting on the hope that once Lily got past the tiny baby stage and turned cute as all get-out, Pamala might at least try to show up and be a mother occasionally. But he'd thought wrong. He'd raged against Pamala's coldhearted betrayal of her own child, but there had been nothing he could do.

He'd been in the mood to go up against someone his own size, and Bruiser had seemed like a creature who was more than willing to meet the challenge. He and the horse had ridden the hills, fighting each other, each one half-crazy and wild. Although there was evidence that the big horse had been abused at one time—there were scars on his back and flanks—he and Noah were a match. They had ended that long ride with an understanding, a wary respect for each other, but Bruiser didn't tolerate anyone else. As big as he was and with that surely volatile history, he was too dangerous to keep on a ranch with a young child who promised to grow up unpredictable.

Noah already had misgivings about his abilities as a parent. He'd made mistakes, he'd failed Lily on many occasions and in many ways, and worst of all, he hadn't been able to stop Pamala from leaving his little girl. But he meant to do better, to be as good a father as he could, so selling Bruiser should have been an easy call. He didn't know why he hadn't done it already, but now he was going to have to. Apparently Ivy Seacrest was going to force his hand.

Again. Noah frowned. He rounded the barn…and came upon Ivy in the corral brushing Bruiser's coat. The huge black creature looked more than a little nervous.

"Ivy," Noah said softly.

She raised her head, looking almost as wary as Bruiser. Like some wild creature who had been abused and expected to be abused again.

"Shh," she said, and she soothed her hand over the big horse's side.

Bruiser shivered, and Noah's breath nearly stopped. "For God's sake, Ivy, step away from the horse. Slowly. Quietly."

"He's not going to hurt me." She leaned closer to the horse.

"He's not a lamb, Ivy. He's big and muscular and easy to anger and—"

He stopped midthought when she smiled. The maddening woman was wedged up against the massive bulk of a nervous horse—and she was smiling. "What on earth are you smiling about?"

"Big, muscular, easy to anger," she said. "Sounds like you."

Suddenly he wanted to smile, too, and he would have if he hadn't still been worried about her safety.

"I mean it, Ivy. Bruiser isn't just any horse."

"I know," she said sadly, tracing a scar that ran down Bruiser's back. "He's been hurt." Her voice nearly broke, but as she ran her hand over the animal, Bruiser whickered softly. He turned his head toward her and nudged her shoulder. Gently. He shivered again, and now Noah could see that Bruiser's expression was anything but angry. That shiver hadn't been nerves. He liked having Ivy pet him.

"You sly devil," Noah said to the animal. "What do you know about that? It seems that my unpredictable, angry horse likes you, Ivy." *He's got something in common with Brody,* Noah thought.

"He just likes someone who understands and trusts him." She stared at him with those big, innocent-looking blue eyes that weren't innocent at all. She was trying to school him, and her point was clear.

Now Noah couldn't keep from smiling. "I don't distrust you." It was more like himself he didn't trust. Around her. She was far too attractive, and he was not a man who could afford to be attracted indiscriminately anymore. Still, he couldn't stop smiling at her attitude.

"You don't distrust me, but you're not hiring me," she pointed out.

"Yes, I am."

"You are?" Her voice was so hopeful and— She obviously pushed hard against Bruiser, who whickered and sidestepped.

"Dammit, Ivy, get out of there."

"I told you...he won't—"

"I know what you told me, but I want you out of there."

She raised her chin. Tall as she was, Bruiser dwarfed her height. Noah almost said "Please." That wouldn't be smart under the circumstances. A boss didn't plead with his employees.

"Are you working for me or not?" he asked, crossing his arms over his chest.

"Yes." And giving Bruiser a hug—a hug, for heaven's sake!—she climbed over the fence and dropped lightly to the ground beside Noah. "I'm working for you. What do you want me to do first?"

Her vault over the fence had left her standing mere inches from him, so close that if he leaned forward he could place his lips against her forehead, tangle himself in that tawny hair.

What do I want you to do? Let me touch you or...no...I want you to step away, dammit! he thought. He almost stepped back himself, fearful that he might put thoughts to deeds and actually touch her. Instead, he cleared his throat. "Tomorrow will be soon enough to start work. For now I'll introduce you to everyone."

"I've met Brody." Oh, yeah, he definitely knew that. Brody was going to be laughing...when he wasn't drooling. Noah was going to have to make some rules about how Ivy was to be treated. By all of them.

He introduced her to Darrell.

"Delighted, Ivy," Darrell said with a smile that Noah thought was much too wide.

"Come on," Noah said, barely giving Ivy time to answer. "Let's go to the house."

Ivy stopped in her tracks. "Oh. No."

Did she think...surely she didn't think... "We won't be alone," he explained.

She blinked and tilted her head back to look into his eyes. "I didn't think that. I just...your family will be there."

"There's just me and my daughter, Lily, and my housekeeper and babysitter, Marta. You'll be in contact with them if you're working here."

She blanched. "I...my father never had any workers. I hadn't thought...I thought I would just work outside with the men. I don't need to meet your daughter."

Something hard and flinty took shape within Noah. Pamala had not wanted children. She'd hated everything associated with her pregnancy and she'd barely looked at Lily after she'd been born. Within days, Pamala had gone. Off to California looking for something better. For the limelight. Away from her baby.

"You don't like children." He couldn't keep the edge from his voice.

But when she looked up this time, her eyes were so... *anguished* was the first word that came to mind.

"I don't dislike children," she whispered. "I need to go home now. I'll be back bright and early tomorrow. To work. Outside."

Then she fled.

Noah stood there wondering what he had done, what he had gotten all of them into. For sure it wasn't anything good.

In the middle of the night he woke from a dream. He'd been plunging his fingers into Ivy's hair, framing her face with his hands, kissing her and staring into those blue eyes.

This time they hadn't been anguished. They'd been filled with passion.

But none of that was real. The reality was that Ivy Seacrest didn't want to be near his Lily.

Finding out why would involve getting to know Ivy better, and he didn't intend to do that. Just as soon as Ed was able to get around without crutches, he'd pay her off handsomely and send her on her way.

No more night dreams of her. He hoped.

CHAPTER THREE

IVY IMMERSED HERSELF IN ranch work as if she really enjoyed it. She drove herself relentlessly. By the end of the first morning the pretty, crisp scarf she'd been unable to resist fastening at her neck was wilted. She was muddy and worn and she had a long scratch on her hand, the result of catching her glove on barbed wire, which tore it off and bit into her skin. Still, there was a sense that she was accomplishing something, closer to her goal of paying her debts, leaving her past and Tallula behind and getting on with her life.

That was a good thing. Of course, she knew darn well that good things didn't last forever, and sure enough, right when she had just got knocked on her butt by a cow and had landed in a pile of muck, she looked up to find herself staring into Noah's amber eyes.

"Need a hand?" he asked, reaching out.

She stared at his big, manly hand and knew that touching him would be a mistake. She'd already realized that he was just too potent for her. But she was his employee. He was just offering what he would offer to Brody or Darrell if either of them had landed on their backsides. Saying no to a gesture of goodwill would make something more of this than the situation merited.

She reached out, felt his hand close around hers, big and

strong. She felt the kick of awareness, the heat that pooled in her body.

"Thank you," she somehow managed to say once she was on her feet and, once again, standing much too close to the man. What was wrong with her lately, anyway? It must just be the effect of being back in a place she'd thought she had left behind long ago. She was ten years older, but nothing had changed.

Except Noah is much more potent than I remember. Ivy wanted to scream at the thought. Instead, she backed off a step and put her shaking hands behind her back.

"You okay?" he asked. "I didn't think she nudged you that hard, but you're pretty slight. Easily hurt."

Ivy chuckled. "Still trying to talk me out of working for you? Too late. You've given me a job, and I'm not going to lose it."

"I saw what you were doing, trying to convince that stubborn cow to accept her calf. She's not too thrilled that you're trying to turn her into a mama."

"Poor little thing. Every time he gets close, she kicks out at him. He's almost too scared to try anymore. But I'm not giving up. This is going to be a love relationship before I'm through."

He shook his head, muttering something about "love relationship" and "city-girl nonsense." He turned to walk away, then swung back.

"Go up to the house and tell Marta you need a change of clothes. There are some things…my wife didn't take everything when she left. I'm sure there are some jeans you can fit into."

Ivy could see that he didn't like talking about his ex-wife. Well, who could blame him? She didn't know anything about Noah's situation, but the words *when she left* were pretty telling. As for his suggestion that she go up to the house? Panic began to beat within her chest.

"I'm fine," she said.

"Ivy," he drawled.

"Noah," she drawled right back.

"I expect my employees to be sensible. You're not acting sensible. Brody and Darrell live on the ranch, and all their things are here, so there's no problem if they need to clean up. You've got nothing here."

Which said a whole lot about her situation in Tallula. She was an outsider, and she *did* have nothing here. Not just on this ranch, but in this whole region. But Noah had given her a job. He was trying to be nice. And she *was* a mess, with a half day of chores still to go. All she had to do was go to the house, quickly change and get back to work. The little girl might not even be around.

"Thank you for offering," she said. "I should remember to leave some clothes here in future." And with great determination, ignoring the tortured pounding of her heart, she started toward the house.

Noah's hand on her arm stopped her. The man must walk like a cougar. She hadn't even heard him coming. She looked up into his eyes.

"What exactly is it about my daughter that bothers you so much?"

They stood there, connected, their eyes locked for several seconds. Then Ivy blinked.

"How much time do you spend on this ranch, Noah?"

He raised one dark eyebrow. "Most of it. Why?"

"I see. Well, that explains things."

He looked perplexed. "Maybe you should explain to me."

She took a deep breath. "You know that I became a model after I left here?"

"Of course. Everybody knows that."

"But you don't know anything about me beyond that."

"I've been a bit busy. I must have let my copy of *Elle* expire."

"Oh, that was wicked, Noah."

"I try."

Ivy almost smiled, except…now came the tough part. She hesitated, then opened her mouth to speak.

He shook his head. "I don't know anything, Ivy, because I don't tune in to gossip. Plus…I really had no right to ask that question. You're here to work, and your skills and dependability are all that matter. I shouldn't have gone all Papa Bear on you and asked. I retract my question."

Somehow that made it easier. "No, I want to explain. I don't want you to think that I dislike her. It's just—when I told you that modeling wasn't an option anymore… I was in a car accident a couple of years ago. That's where I got these scars." She touched her face. Some days she missed the profession she'd loved, but there were things so much more important than being pretty. She would lose more, give more, if only…

"My husband was killed," she rushed on, "and…and my little boy was…he was, too. So please don't think I have anything against your Lily, Noah. It's not that at all. I just…" She bit down to keep her lips from trembling.

"Ivy, I'm—damn, I'm sorry. I didn't mean to pry." He slid his hand up her arm and across her cheek. He cupped her jaw in his palm. "I'm so sorry. Next time you just tell me to shut up."

Ivy felt as if her body was being taken to another plane. She was aware of every inch of her skin Noah touched. And his concern—that rough quality in his voice—made her want to lean close, touch him, too. She hadn't had anyone other than doctors touch her in two years.

That thought stopped everything. If she reacted to the sensation of Noah's skin against her own, it was just because this was the first time. She struggled for something smart-mouthed to say, anything to distract her attention from the physical contact between them. What had he said to her?

She found a tiny half smile somewhere. "I've never had a boss tell me that I should tell him to shut up."

"You've probably never had a boss who made such a boneheaded misstep."

Finally she found her footing and gave him a real, whole smile. "You've clearly never been a model if you think that."

The laugh that emanated from his body traveled through his skin, the vibration pulsing in his fingers that were still touching her face. As if he realized what he was doing to her, he lowered his arm. "Yeah, no modeling for a rough guy like me."

Although, in her mind, he could name his price if he went into modeling. Women would empty their piggy banks just to get him to take his shirt off.

"I'll just go to the house and get something for you," he said. "There's an empty crew house over the rise. It's not much, but you can use it while you're here."

"I don't like acting weak," she confessed.

"Lady, you hugged Bruiser. You took a shove from a cow that weighs ten times what you do. *Weak* is not a word I'd use with you."

"What words would you use with me?" *Where had that come from?* "That came out wrong. Let's just not go there," she corrected.

"Too late," he said with a wink. "I have three words to describe you right now. *Stubborn, sassy* and...*in need of clean jeans.*"

"That's more than three words."

He chuckled. "Roll with it. Ranching demands flexibility."

Noah turned to leave. Then he quickly turned back. "You're bound to run across her now and then while you're here. Can you handle it?"

Ivy nodded tightly. "I'm so sorry about this, Noah. I'm sure your child is sweet, and I would never want to do anything that would hurt her. I just…I'm still working things through, and right now…"

He held up a hand. "You don't have to explain. If anything happened to Lily, I'd be insane. Everything I do, say or am right now and for the next twenty years or so revolves around her. Every decision I make deals with her. I never forget that, so while I can't possibly put myself in your shoes, I can understand why being around her is a problem for you. I—you know how temporary this job is, don't you?"

"Yes. I don't need it to be anything else. I'm not staying."

"Good. I can't and won't hide my child away, but since you won't be here long, we can make concessions that wouldn't work out if you were long-term. What I'm saying is that I'll do my best to make any contact between you as brief as possible. Will that work for you?"

"Yes."

She would make it work. Somehow she would manage to make all of this work.

And she would not think of Noah as anything other than her boss. She definitely wouldn't allow herself to remember how much she had liked having his fingers against her skin.

"Yeah, I'll get right to *not* remembering that," she muttered to herself as he strode toward the house and she tried *not* noticing how long and strong his legs were.

Why had she ever imagined that working for Noah would be smart?

Noah carried the jeans out to Ivy. *Just pretend you don't even know that in a few minutes she's going to slip out of her clothes and pour her long, slender body into these, Ballenger,* he told himself, struggling to do just that.

"They might be a bit short," he told her, his fingertips brushing hers as he handed them over. A zing of male awareness ricocheted through his body at the touch. *Ignore that,* he ordered himself.

"I'm sure they'll be fine. Thank you," she said softly.

"Here, I'll show you the cottage. It's been empty for a while, so I'm not too sure how things look inside."

They looked pretty bad. When he opened the door and saw the layer of dust and the sad and shabby furnishings, the first thought he had was that she had been a model. This would look like a hovel to her.

"It needs work," he said, stating the obvious.

"I like work."

"Well, then, you're going to love this place." He stepped past her to pull open a shade, and as he did, his body brushed hers. Was that hiss of awareness coming from him or from her?

Noah looked into her eyes. He couldn't tell what she was thinking, but he could tell that she wasn't unaffected by him.

Too bad. The lady's off-limits. "I'll just let you get to…"

Undressing.

"Business," he said, hoping that his voice didn't sound hoarse. "And I'll get back to mine."

Probably best to leave Ivy to Brody's care, he thought, heading back to the house. But something stubborn and strong inside him didn't like that idea.

So deal with it. He'd obviously been on the ranch too long; his reaction to her was beyond hot. But there was nothing he could do about that. He and Ivy had a deal. He would keep Lily away from her, and Ivy would leave as soon as this job ran out.

That thought strengthened him. He'd been an idiot before, but all of that was pre-Lily. There were serious, long-term consequences to his actions now. He couldn't afford to do anything stupid.

Ivy Seacrest would be just another hand to him from now on. The fact that she made him break out in a cold sweat couldn't matter.

Three days passed, and Ivy tried to work and not pay attention to anything else going on around the ranch. She tried not to notice her aching muscles or the fact that her ranching skills were rusty. She especially tried not to remember how she had reacted to Noah in that split-second brush of his body against hers when he had moved to open the shades.

"Damn, damn, damn," she muttered beneath her breath. For two long years she had not had one whit of an interest in men. Life had jerked her around too much and all the bad times had boiled down to her dealings with men who had ruined her life—her father who had destroyed her mother with his blind, obsessive devotion to his ranch, and her husband, Alden, whose obsessions that blinded him to others' feelings had destroyed everything else that had mattered to her. She would never get involved with another man who wore blinders, and it was clear that Noah did.

That comment about *Elle* magazine had been funny,

but it had obviously also been true. Despite his comment about gossip, he had to have been out roaming the range not to have known anything about her past, given the way the paparazzi had covered her accident.

Or maybe he'd been mourning the loss of his wife, she thought. But even that was evidence of how much he cared about this ranch. She'd heard that his ex-wife had left because she hated the ranch. Yet Noah had stayed. He'd let her go.

That was none of her business, but it was just impossible to dodge. The other day when she'd shown up wearing the too-short jeans, Darrell's eyebrows had risen.

"Noah let you wear Pamala's pants?"

The pants were a bit loose around the waist, but Ivy had suddenly felt as if they were too tight. She'd wondered if Noah would look at her and think of his Pamala.

Brody had let out a low whistle. "They look way better on you, Ivy, even though they're a bit high on your boots. But—damn!—I'm surprised those are even still around. I would have thought Noah would have burned those things. She sure burned *him.* She hated Ballenger Ranch like fire hates water."

Ever since then, Ivy had tried not to wonder about the man who'd let his wife walk while he stayed at the ranch. It wasn't any of her business, but she was still glad she knew. It would make it easier to think of Noah not as a man but as a man she couldn't want. Actually, it would be best not to think of him at all, but that was impossible—a truth that was driven home when she found out that the following morning she would need to ride out on a search for lost cattle. Roping would be involved. Noah would be there.

Her courage nearly failed her. She'd never been good with a rope and hadn't had much experience with one. Her less than stellar performance might convince Noah that he'd made a mistake hiring her. So at the end of the day she took a rope and, moving as far away from the house as she could, she practiced, using a bale of hay with a stick jammed into it. Time and again, Ivy swung the rope, but without much success. Anxiety made her clumsy. She had told Noah she would be a good hand. What would he say when she couldn't even hit her targets?

Biting her lip, she turned and stared off into the distance, hands on her hips. Frustration nearly paralyzed her, but standing there worrying wasn't helping. "Stop being such a coward, Seacrest," she muttered to herself. "Just keep trying." She turned back to her task.

"You're swinging too high to the right, and the loop you're using is too big for you."

Finishing her turn in a rush, Ivy stared at Noah, who was standing less than twenty feet away and moving closer.

"How—how long have you been watching me?"

"Long enough to see the problem."

To see that she couldn't even hit an immobile stick, much less a moving animal. "I'll practice. I'll be better by morning."

He gave her a long, assessing stare and shook his head. "I've got a dummy steer that will work better than that stick. I'll show you how to use it another day. Tomorrow we'll do the run without you."

No, no, no, ran through her mind. He would lose respect for her. So would Brody and Darrell. A hand who couldn't carry her weight was a liability, not a help. "I'll make the adjustments you suggested. Noah, I know this isn't my call, but…I want to be there tomorrow. I'll learn. I won't be deadweight." She had very little left in the world. She couldn't afford to lose this job…or her pride.

But she could see that he didn't believe her. And why should he? If he'd seen her repeatedly miss the target, he had to be thinking she'd be more of a hindrance than a help.

"I'll keep practicing tonight until I have it," she said. And when he didn't answer her right away... "Please," she managed to whisper as heat flooded her face.

Noah swore. "Why didn't your father teach you to rope?"

"I guess...he wasn't very good at it himself."

Noah gave a terse nod. He turned and started walking.

"Noah?"

"Don't move. I'll be back," he said.

A few minutes later he returned with a contraption that looked like a plastic steer's head on a metal body. "All right. Let's do it," he said.

Something like relief and gratitude mixed with fear swooshed through Ivy. She concentrated hard as she twirled the rope, knowing her loop was too wobbly and uncertain.

Noah stepped to her side. "Like this," he said, gently grasping her hand and guiding her arm. "Keep the loop of the rope open and bring it across your body this way as you twirl it. Nice, easy motions. Steady." But she didn't feel at all steady. Noah was trying to help her, but the closeness of his big hard body, the warmth of his touch as his arm came around her and crossed her body, brushing against her, made it difficult to breathe or think. She looked up at him over her shoulder and for a moment the rope stopped moving as he stared back at her, their hands joined.

"That's the basic movement," he said, letting her go and stepping away. "Now you try on your own."

She twirled the rope, awkwardly at first.

"The back of your hand will almost touch your mouth as it comes around," he said, demonstrating with his own rope. "When you release the rope here," he said, showing her, "the momentum of your arm finishing the turn and your hand pointing this way will send the rope right over the steer's horns." Breaking the instructions down into simple steps, Noah finally made it make sense for Ivy as she watched him rope the dummy steer.

"Are you ready to try again?" he asked.

Ivy nodded, more determined than ever. For the first time she felt hopeful that she could master this skill. She might be awkward, but with Noah's help, she understood the mechanics of the process. Twirling her loop, keeping it open, she paid attention to her hand and to the loop as she released it. It fell short, and she was disappointed, but it was close. Her earlier attempts hadn't been. She sucked in her lip, her brow furrowing.

"Again," he said.

Ivy twirled the rope again. Miss. Throw. Miss. Throw. This time it landed neatly over the horns.

"Yes!" she said, grinning at Noah. "That's one. It was a good one, too, wasn't it?"

He laughed. "It was a sweet little toss. A winner."

But one toss standing on the ground wouldn't be good enough for tomorrow's task. "Thank you," Ivy said. "I—you can go now. I'm just going to keep practicing until I'm consistent."

He raised a brow. "It's been a long day, and tomorrow will come early. You should rest. You know, there are plenty of cowboys who aren't especially good ropers."

And those cowboys sometimes got passed over for better ones. "I'm not going to be that kind," Ivy said. She tossed the rope again. And again. Over and over, , until she could land it most of the time. By now Noah was leaning against the fence and watching her with a lazy-cat smile on his face.

"What?" she asked.

"Don't your batteries ever run down?"

"Not when I need to get something done."

"Well, you're done now. Your arm's going to be sore."

"But tomorrow I'll be on a horse. I need to try it on a horse."

"Ivy…"

"Noah…just a few times, so that I won't be nervous tomorrow?"

"One or both of us will fall off the horse asleep tomorrow if we don't finish up here soon," he muttered, but he led her to Binny, a sweet little palomino. "She's gentle and patient."

Which was a good thing. Roping from horseback was more complicated than being on foot. Ivy didn't really reach proficiency, but she was beginning to be afraid that Noah was right. They both had to work tomorrow, and… he had a child waiting. The thought made Ivy feel guilty. She sighed, turning in the saddle to apologize to Noah for keeping him out so late.

"You *are* tired," he said, misinterpreting her sigh. "That's enough, Ivy." With that, he reached up and plucked her from Binny's back, sliding her to the ground. "Bed," he said.

She blinked. His hands were still around her waist. He was so close. She was still tingling from the contact, and the word *bed* hung between them.

Noah swore, and not beneath his breath this time. He let her go. "Don't argue with me anymore today, Ivy. Just go." He was obviously not any happier than she was at the arc of electricity that had passed between them.

Ivy's breathing was still erratic. "Okay," she said in a rush. "I'm done. Don't worry."

But she worried for a long time before she fell asleep. If she were smart, she'd give Noah a wide berth from now on...even if she couldn't stop thinking about how his hands had felt on her.

Apparently Noah had been thinking the same thing, because the next day he worked mostly with Darrell and assigned her to Brody. The day passed and the one after that. She and Noah spoke very little other than basic greetings. Most of her orders came through Brody.

Still, whenever she saw Noah in the distance—working, riding, lifting his daughter onto his shoulders—something about him made her stop and look.

On the third day Ivy was gathering equipment to go help Darrell repair a windmill when she saw Noah heading toward the house. The door flew open, and Lily came tumbling out, running in that frantic, wobbly way that two-year-olds run.

"Da!" she squealed, raising her arms, confident that her daddy would pick her up.

"Hey, pumpkin, how's my girl? Did you get away from Marta?" Noah scooped up the tiny child and swung her into his arms right against his chest.

Ivy couldn't turn away. She couldn't move. She couldn't stop thinking about Bo's toddler laughter that she had never heard. And yet that wasn't this child's or this man's fault.

She stared, even though the pain cut right through her, razor sharp, leaving a trail of desolation she couldn't control. It came upon her suddenly, tracking her down, forcing her to remember that she would never, ever get to hear Bo laugh. *Never.*

Tears slipped down her cheeks, and she swiped them away. She fought the keening wail that threatened to escape her. Then Noah began to turn.

Ivy ran. She stumbled into the toolshed, scrubbed her face with her hands and began rummaging through the tools, blindly looking for…something. She didn't even know what she was looking for.

The shadow that fell over her told her that he was standing in the doorway. "Be right there," she said, hoping that her voice didn't sound too thick.

"Ivy." He knew. He'd seen.

"I just have to get a few tools. Darrell and I are going to fix the windmill out on Jessup Flats. Darrell's waiting."

"Ivy, I'm sorry."

She turned, pushing her chin high. "Don't be. She's a sweet little girl. She's yours. The fact that I lost my son—that doesn't mean you should apologize for having a daughter."

"I'm not." He came into the room.

No. Don't, she thought. *I'm not strong right now. I need to get my feisty back on so no one can see the cracks.* Hiding the cracks was all that had gotten her through most of her life.

"Then there's nothing to apologize for," she said. "Don't be silly."

"I'm never silly." He said the word as if he didn't know the meaning. She had to admit that she had desperately pulled that one out of a hat, trying to change the tone in a wild stab at regaining her composure and her cool. Models didn't show emotion unless directed to.

But I'm not a model anymore.

Maybe not, but she still lived by those rules. "It's been a long time since I helped fix a windmill. Has the technology changed?" she asked, peering into the tool bin.

"Not around here." He reached past her, scooped up a pipe wrench and handed it to her. When both their hands were on the tool, he didn't let go. "I thought you were away from the house, with Brody. I'm sorry for your loss, Ivy."

Okay, he was going to insist on being nice, on doing the polite thing. Maybe that would make it easier. All she had to do was be polite right back and he would go. She wouldn't have to keep wishing that he would touch her. Noah—with his child when she could *not* be around children and with his ranch when she could *not* live on a ranch—was the worst man on earth for her. But…she knew how to politely talk her way out of a situation, didn't she?

"Thank you. I appreciate that," she said. "It helps."

He uttered a curse word that she was pretty darn sure he never used around Lily. "It doesn't help. Even a brute like me knows that, Ivy. So…has anything helped?"

Ah, there was her out. "Work. Work helps."

"Then I guess I'd better let you go." But he didn't let go of the wrench.

"Noah?"

"What?"

Her mind was a jumble. He was so close. She was so… darn, he was so close. She glanced down at their fingers, only inches away from each other. His gaze followed hers. "I don't like this…this physical stuff messing with my job," she said, tugging on the wrench. "So why don't you just kiss me so we can get it over with?"

Ivy's suggestion shocked even her. Well, she wasn't exactly thinking straight right now. And why not kiss the man? Everyone in town seemed to think she had come to Tallula on a mission to collect men anyway. Why not live up to their expectations, spit in their eyes the way she always had? Her city-bred parents had been snooty to the people of Tallula, and Ivy had always been an outsider, long before she'd left and become an actual outsider. She'd learned to tough it out, act the part. Slipping back into that persona would probably be easy enough.

"Or better yet, *I'll* kiss you," she said. She rose on her toes, grasped Noah's shirt and planted one quick kiss on his lips.

Simple. Easy. *No. Not either of those. At all.* Noah's lips were warm; his masculine scent surrounded her; his big body made her want to curl closer.

Panic ensued, and Ivy rushed toward the door before she could do something stupid…like let Noah see how that kiss had affected her. "Now," she said as nonchalantly as she could, "we've got that behind us, so we can totally forget this ever happened and get on with our lives. And don't ever apologize to me again for loving your daughter."

She fled, her lips burning, her cheeks on fire. And, she soon realized, she had left without a single tool. What on earth would she tell Darrell?

She didn't know…or care. She had kissed Noah Ballenger. Was she totally insane?

"Yes," she whispered. "But at least he isn't pitying me right now."

He was probably getting ready to fire her butt.

CHAPTER FOUR

NOAH FELT LIKE a restless lion who'd been prowling solo for months and had just realized that there was a female in the vicinity.

Ivy would probably hate that comparison. That rigid backbone, determined chin and all that sass were hard evidence that she had a boatload of pride. And she was doing her damnedest to hang on to it. She liked to play tough, to keep people off guard so that they couldn't see the pain she was carrying. Even someone like him who was a heck of a lot better with horses than with women could see that. That was why she'd kissed him, wasn't it? To distract him from feeling sorry for her.

Well, it had certainly worked. For a few minutes his entire body had flamed. His brain cells had fried. Every nerve ending on his body had reacted. That mouth, that silky, soft mouth that tasted of peppermint and some indefinable sweetness that was hers alone had left him wanting to chase her down, pull her against his body and plunder that mouth again.

That would have been incredibly dumb. She had been right. The sparks had been flying between them from the first, but they needed to get that out of the way, because there could be *nothing* between them.

She couldn't even look at Lily. And he would never

allow Lily to be hurt again. He would never get tangled up with anyone who would desert his child.

Ivy and her luscious lips were off-limits. And he would just have to suck it up and take it. And consider himself lucky that he had gotten one taste.

"I saw you kiss Ivy." Brody's voice came from behind him.

Oh, hell, Noah thought. He couldn't even defend himself. He didn't want Brody to know that it was Ivy who had done the kissing, especially since she'd kissed him only to get rid of him. Hadn't the woman been hurt enough?

"You didn't see anything," Noah said. "It was nothing."

"*Nothing* sure looked hot."

"Nothing is ever going to happen again," Noah reiterated. But he wondered if he was trying to convince Brody or himself.

Well, she had certainly done it, Ivy thought. Kissing Noah had seemed like a good idea at the time. She'd been sizzling every time he got near and she had thought that kissing him would kill two birds with one stone. It would get him to stop pitying her for losing her child while he still had his, and it would release the physical tension that had been building between them.

"Wrong on at least one count," she whispered. Now that she'd felt Noah's mouth beneath hers, she wanted to kiss him again. She wanted him to kiss *her,* and she wanted… she looked down at her hands. She wanted to touch him.

"Argh!" she said, rubbing a cloth over the kitchen counter of the crew house. She had moved out of her old home that was filled with ghosts and bad memories. The spartan little cottage suited her. There were no memories here.

Under other circumstances and on any other day, it would have been perfect.

Today this house and the ranch simply reminded her of Noah, the last person she needed to be thinking about. He couldn't be in her plans; she couldn't be in his.

She needed to get away, and her parents' house wasn't a good choice. Where could she go?

Well, she *did* need to pick up a few things, and playing "bad Ivy" with the townspeople would at least take her mind off Noah. There would be tension, but the tension in Tallula would be the kind she could handle.

Borrowing the old ranch pickup that Brody had told her she could use, she headed for Tallula, parked and walked into a small department store. As she entered, several people turned toward her.

Immediately a salesclerk rushed up. "Ms. Seacrest, may I help you? That is…we don't carry too many fancy things…."

"Nothing a model would wear," another woman said, her tone judgmental. Ivy recognized the woman. She'd been a pretty girl, but the boy she'd liked had been fixated on Ivy. Now, remembering the ache she felt every time she witnessed the closeness between Noah and his daughter, closeness that had been torn away from her, Ivy felt a twinge of responsibility toward the woman and dismissed her snooty remarks. Maybe she was married and the marriage wasn't going well. Maybe she and her husband had fought this morning. Maybe she was worried that Ivy would overshadow her again and steal her happiness.

So even though her first reaction as a teenager would have been to put up her chin and say something smart, or to act cool and unmoved, Ivy decided to take a different tack, to try to be nice in the face of nastiness.

"It's okay. I'm sure you have exactly what I need," she said. "I'll look around until I find what I want."

Silence settled in. Ivy's heart thudded. She reminded herself that she had always been an outsider here and always would be. And why should she care, when she wasn't staying?

She drifted over to a rack of cotton work shirts, then found some inexpensive but pretty scarves, looking up to see the belligerent woman still staring at her. What had the woman's name been? Oh, yes, Sandra. The other women had nodded curtly at Ivy's speech, and one or two had even smiled a little, but not this one. Clearly, Ivy's speech hadn't mollified Sandra.

Ivy soon found out why. There was a small coffee shop in the store, and a few of the women wandered over there. Whispering ensued. A few looks were cast Ivy's way.

Finally one woman separated from the rest and approached Ivy. "I know we haven't met. I didn't live here back when you did. I married into Tallula," the woman said. "I'm Alicia Kendall." She held out her hand.

Ivy blinked and shook her hand. "It's nice to meet you, Alicia."

"Ask her about Noah," a woman called.

Ivy's heart started thudding. The women of the town had decided that she was here to mine men. Did they think she was trying to seduce Noah?

"What do you want to know?" she asked, raising her chin defensively and looking directly at the woman who had asked the question.

For half a second the woman looked embarrassed, but then she shrugged. "What's he up to? He almost never comes to town. You can't blame a single woman for being interested in what a good-looking single man is doing. I mean…can you? Don't you think he's handsome?"

Ivy hesitated. "Is this a test?" she finally asked.

The woman blinked, and Ivy gave her a slow smile. "Sorry. Bad habit," Ivy said. "I guess I was a bit of a smart mouth when I lived here, wasn't I?"

"More standoffish, I'd say," another woman said, looking down her nose a bit. "Since you asked."

Was this the strangest conversation? Ivy wondered. She'd been here for several days before being hired, and no one had wanted anything to do with her. She had wanted nothing to do with them. There was friction in the air. So... why was she half enjoying this exchange?

But she knew. When she'd lived here, she'd always felt trapped, a fish out of water...or maybe a fish frantically swimming in circles in a teacup. Then, when she returned and had been trying to find work, she'd been scared. But now that Noah had hired her...well, she knew she wasn't staying. She had a job; she wasn't trapped. She could relax a bit, she decided. Interact.

"Fair enough," she agreed. "I was standoffish." She'd never been good at the up-close-and-personal stuff, because her home hadn't been that way. "But I'm afraid I can't tell you much about Noah. I just work for him. I hang with the hands."

That seemed to satisfy most of the women. But they didn't drop the topic of Noah. "It's a shame he never brings Lily to town," one woman said.

"A child should have contact with other children."

"A man shouldn't be alone," Sandra said. "Noah deserves a good woman, his own kind." She looked at Ivy, and Ivy was tempted to hold up her hands as if to say *This has nothing to do with me*. But she remembered that kiss. She just couldn't forget that kiss.

Another woman laughed. "As if he couldn't have one if he wanted. Give it up, Sandra. He'll marry when he wants to. Lily, now, she's another story. She's growing up alone on a ranch with no other kid contact. That's wrong."

"Are you going to tell Noah that?" Alicia asked.

"Tell Noah how to raise his daughter? I'd sooner tell the devil that he should have air-conditioning in hell. Some things you just don't do if you don't want to have your head bitten off."

"I think he should bring her to town," Sandra suddenly said.

"You just want Noah here so you can slobber over him."

Someone else laughed. "It *would* be nice to have the chance to gaze on Noah now and then. Someday he might get over Pamala, but if he doesn't come to town, he won't even think about one of us. And we can't just make up some excuse to go see *him,* either. He'd see right through that."

There was a sudden silence, and Ivy looked up to see several speculative glances on her. What was that about? Were they looking at her scars? Had they finally noticed the obvious?

Ivy didn't know, but she once again felt like an outsider. *I don't care. It doesn't matter,* she reminded herself. She'd be gone soon enough.

For now, she just wanted to escape. She quickly paid for her things and headed for the door.

"Goodbye, Ivy," someone called out, to her surprise.

Ivy turned and saw Alicia's encouraging smile. Several more women called goodbye, albeit with less enthusiasm.

"Goodbye," Ivy said quietly. "I—I guess I'll be seeing you."

"Oh, you will," Sandra said, without smiling. "Tell Noah that Sandra says hello."

Ivy managed to get out the door, but for some reason she didn't want to understand, she didn't tell Sandra that she would tell Noah anything.

Because I'm staying away from him as much as I can, she told herself. But she knew that that wasn't the reason. Sandra wanted to be the next Mrs. Ballenger, and while Ivy knew that she and Noah were all wrong for each other, she didn't think Sandra was right for him, either.

Or maybe she just didn't want to think about Noah's lips pressed against Sandra's.

"And maybe you just better forget that kiss," she muttered to herself. But she knew that she wouldn't.

It had been two days since Ivy had gone into town. Noah hadn't fired her for being insubordinate or for kissing the boss, but he *had* kept his distance. That didn't mean she wasn't totally aware of his whereabouts every minute. At times she even thought she felt his amber gaze on her, but when she turned around, he was always involved in some chore.

Still, every time, her heart started to thud…too hard.

She didn't miss what was going on with Noah and his daughter, either. Despite her efforts to ignore Lily, the little girl's laugh carried, her soft lisping voice touched a chord in Ivy's heart and…well, it was wrong to keep a child cooped up, so she did her best to remain at a distance so that Lily could run and play freely and Noah wouldn't feel guilty.

But the women's words about Noah and Lily kept running through her head, and not just the stuff about how incredibly hot Noah was, but the fact that he stayed on the ranch and never took Lily to town to play with other children.

She's only two, Ivy thought. *And what do you know about parenting?*

"It's none of your business," she muttered.

"Are you talking to me?"

Ivy looked up and saw Noah standing in front of her. She had been looking down at the ground as she walked, lost in her thoughts, but here he was, shirt off, a grease smear on his shoulder and a spark-plug wrench in his hand. He was standing next to the old truck she drove. The hood was open.

"Did I break it?" she asked.

He laughed, and deep dimples appeared in his cheeks. His dark hair had fallen over his forehead. He was a mess, and she had never seen anything she wanted her hands on so much in her entire life. "It breaks all by itself. Regularly. Make sure you carry a phone when you're driving."

"I know a few things about cars," she said. "May I help?" Why on earth had she offered?

But she knew. She *knew*. She wanted to be close to that beautiful muscular body. She wanted to be there in case he laughed again. She wasn't any better than Sandra.

Except I don't want to marry him, she thought. *I just want to touch him, maybe look at him a little.*

She was totally pathetic.

"You'll get grease on you," he warned.

"Grease won't kill a person."

"Not the trendiest look for models, though."

"I told you, I don't model anymore." It was getting easier to say those words, even though she sometimes missed the profession where she had fit and felt comfortable. With Noah, she felt...too aware of her body. And his body.

He nodded. "I heard you the first time you told me." But he looked her over carefully, as if examining her for flaws from head to toe. Ivy squirmed. She fought to hold her head high, so that her scars were visible.

"Not buying it," he said. "You carry your head higher than most women do. I've noticed those pretty little scarves you wear, the ones you know darn well will never make it through the day, but you wear them anyway. You'll always be Ivy Seacrest, international model."

He was so wrong. The scars had ruled that out, but she didn't argue. Pointing out her scars only sounded as if she were asking for pity, and pity wasn't what she wanted from Noah. No, she wanted…

A job. Just a job, she told herself. "Just the spark plugs or a full tune-up?" she asked.

"Full. I'm mostly done. Just have to change the oil."

She nodded, grabbed the oil wrench and pan and slid beneath the truck.

"You're pretty handy," Noah conceded.

She chuckled as she drained the oil into the pan. "I told you, I had to learn all this when I was growing up."

"So ranch chores, repairing cars…what else?"

"The usual. Cooking, cleaning, general household maintenance, painting." She left out the bit about nursing an injured mother because her father wouldn't pay for a doctor. That wasn't for sharing.

"All that and you went to school, too."

"They don't call us supermodels for nothing," she said, trying to tease because she was afraid that he was feeling sorry for her.

"No arguments here. I'm just not sure I want to go that route with—well, I admire your skills, but your days must have been long."

He'd been thinking about what his plans were for Lily, hadn't he? Ivy remembered what the women in town had said.

None of your business. Keep out, she thought. And yet…she slid from beneath the truck, wiping the oil off her hands with a rag. "When I was in town, there were some ladies talking about you."

He raised one dark brow. One dark *sexy* brow. Uh-oh. "What were they saying?"

"You mean, besides the fact that they all want to run naked before you and have your babies?"

"Interesting conversation."

"Just saying that they seemed disappointed that I couldn't give them any hot news about you."

"So you and the ladies in town are tight, eh?"

"Like this," she said, twisting her fingers around each other. "Actually, we're not so tight. I barely know them. At least one of them hates me. None of the others want to be my shopping buddy. Not their fault. I didn't spend a lot of time socializing when I was growing up."

"Understandable. You were fixing cars and herding cattle and painting houses."

"Right." Because he was partially right. Even if she had "fit" with the girls in town, she wouldn't have had time to play. Which brought her back to the topic at hand. The one she wasn't going to go near.

"But I could tell this much from their conversation. They think you're keeping Lily from meeting other kids. They think it's bad for her."

Oh, brother, just shut up, Seacrest.

"I see."

"No, you don't. You think I'm being nosy and—okay, I am being nosy. Lily is…"

"Off-limits."

"Yes."

"And you never wanted to talk about her before."

She still didn't. It hurt too much.

"I know, but—"

"But nothing. No one tells me how to raise my kid."

"I'm not doing that."

"Sounds a lot like that's where you're headed, Ivy."

"Okay, you're right, but…"

"I'll take her around to meet other kids when it's time, but I want her to be grounded here first."

"You're afraid she'll like town better." Like his wife.

A mask came down over his eyes. The discussion was closed. She didn't blame him. She had crossed a line. If Bo were still alive and some…stranger with no experience tried to tell her how to raise him, she'd feel the same way Noah did. Ivy cursed herself for doing something as stupid as trying to advise a real father on how to parent. She felt awkward, embarrassed and angry with herself, so she knelt to return to her task.

"Do you think you know so much more than I do?" Noah asked suddenly.

"No!" The word came out on a harsh whisper. "I know nothing. *Almost* nothing. I know…this one thing. I *lived* this one thing. If you keep her here, she'll eventually feel trapped and grow to hate it. But you're right. It's your call. She *is* only two. There's still time. I think."

Noah swore beneath his breath. "Is that what happened to you? Your daddy trapped you on that ranch of his? I used to hear things, but—" he held out his hands "—I never knew much about the man."

Ivy looked up into his eyes. "The ranch was all he thought about. It was his life, so he made it my life. He didn't like the town or the people, just the ranch. We weren't good neighbors and I felt awkward in school. I felt as if people knew I was a prisoner in my home. I didn't know how to talk to people. I never learned. But you won't do that to Lily. You love her."

"I do. She's everything. And I won't hurt her. I promise. I won't trap her."

His words were soft and solemn. They made her ache, because they felt like…like an apology to her. She nodded and ducked her head. She needed to get back to work, to remember that he was her boss, and only her temporary boss at that.

But before she could slide back under the truck, he knelt beside her. "I'm sorry for what happened to you back then."

Oh, no. Pity again. "Don't be. It made me strong."

"All right. Then I'm glad that you got to escape and had the chance to see the world."

"And I apologize for interfering."

"You were concerned about Lily."

She shrugged. She didn't want to be concerned about Lily. She absolutely could not open that door. The risk of being destroyed was too great.

"Ivy?"

"What?"

"Look at me."

She didn't want to, but if she didn't, he would think she was weak.

"Some of those women have been giving you the cold shoulder, haven't they?"

"They have their reasons."

"I can't think of a single good one. I'll talk to them."

Reaching out, she curved her palm around his bare biceps, clamping down, trying not to notice the sensation of her skin against his. "No."

"It's not right."

"It is what it is. I'll handle things."

"You're my employee. I can't have people mistreating you."

"If you think that you chastising them for not liking me will change their minds, you're totally clueless. Some of them are half in love with you."

He frowned. "Ivy…"

"Noah…please don't. It won't help, and it doesn't matter anyway. I won't be here long enough for it to matter." It was a warning to herself. She didn't want to become one of those women. She didn't want any man having power over her again.

He blew out an exasperated breath. "Only half in love?" he suddenly said.

"What?"

He gave her a slow grin. "The women. Only half in love with me?"

"You're good. Maybe that's why you're the boss."

"Good at what?"

"At turning a topic around. At dispelling tension."

"Maybe. Maybe not." He looked into her eyes, and she saw the fire burning there. Oh, yeah, he was right. There was plenty of tension here.

"I have to be smart," he said. "And not follow my instincts. You understand what I mean?"

How could she not when he glanced down to where her fingers were still curled around his arm? The very sight made her long to slide her hand higher, up his arm, down his chest. Instantly she let go of him.

"People can get hurt," he said. He meant her. Somehow she knew he meant her.

"*I* won't."

"Because you're strong?"

No. She wasn't that strong. "Because I know what happens when a woman lets a man have power over her. I've done it before. My father. My husband. The results were disastrous, so I'm pretty much done with men."

"Pretty much?"

She frowned. "I'm getting there. I want to be completely done, but I'm only human. I still feel desire."

Noah groaned. "I really wish you hadn't said that."

"Why?"

His answer was to swoop in and kiss her. Just once…and once was not enough. Not nearly. Her lips stung, burned, ached. She barely resisted the urge to press against him and return the kiss. In fact, she was leaning into him when she caught herself. And saved herself by quickly picking up her oil wrench and slipping beneath the car.

Fiddling with the car, she fought to calm herself. "Now I'm done," she said.

"With the oil change?"

"With men."

"Good. I'm holding you to your word. I don't trust myself not to touch you again, so I'm just going to have to trust you."

Don't trust me, Ivy thought. But hadn't she just told him that she was strong?

Be strong. Be smart, she thought as she yanked on the wrench and removed the filter. *I will,* she promised. Because if she just stayed away from Noah, banked her paychecks and let the hourglass run out, nothing could happen. Right?

CHAPTER FIVE

NOAH WAS IN THE KITCHEN finishing breakfast with Lily when a car pulled up in front of the house. Mary Sue Morris, who ran the flower shop in town, emerged, wearing a slinky dress that this ranch had never seen the likes of before. Half a minute later she knocked on the door. Had she been one of the women who had criticized his parenting skills?

Marta opened it just as Noah moved away from the window and into the living room. "Mary Sue," he said with a frown. "Problem?"

Her cheeks turned bright pink. "Oh. No. I'm just—I'm looking for Ivy. She was in town the other day, and...well, I need to get to know her better. Is she around?"

Yes. He'd seen her come out of her house a few minutes ago wearing those jeans that fit her long legs and curves perfectly, a white shirt, and a pale blue scarf at her throat that made him want to untie it with his teeth and kiss the tender skin that lay beneath. Darn it, he could not be this way about a woman who would leave, a woman who hated ranching and a woman who was afraid of his child. And yet he was aware of her. Constantly. The sensation of her in his arms, his lips on hers drove him crazy. Constantly.

He glared. Mary Sue smiled at him brightly. What in hell was that about?

"Ivy's working." His voice was gruff.

The woman shrugged. "That's perfectly okay, Noah. It's been so long since you and I talked, anyway."

They had never really talked. And he certainly didn't want to talk now, especially if she was going to bring the conversation around to Lily and his deficiencies as a father.

"It's probably time for Ivy's break," he grumbled. "I'll find her."

"Oh…okay. I'll walk with you."

His frown didn't seem to dissuade her, and as she ran to keep up with him, the darn woman kept talking about how much she'd always wanted to live on a ranch. She kept giggling, which made Noah walk faster.

Still, when he found Ivy cleaning out the horses' stalls, the whole ordeal of listening to Mary Sue giggle was totally worth it. Ivy looked at her dirty clothes and at Mary Sue's slinky dress. Her perfect model's blue-violet eyes widened. Clearly she hadn't been expecting this.

Noah performed the introductions—Ivy didn't seem to have a clue who Mary Sue was—and then he leaned against a nearby railing to see what happened next. He remembered what Ivy had said about the women of the town not liking her, and despite her protestations that he shouldn't interfere, he wasn't leaving until he was sure that Mary Sue would behave herself.

"Well…here you are," Mary Sue said.

"Here I am," Ivy agreed, her brow furrowed in concentration. "Can I help you?" she asked the woman.

For a second Mary Sue looked flustered. "You've been away awhile. I thought we might get reacquainted."

By rights Noah should be upset that Mary Sue was interrupting the work day, but his curiosity about why the woman was here when Ivy had intimated that no one liked her trumped his irritation.

"It's break time. Go. Talk," Noah said, even though work time hadn't started that long ago.

His comment sent Ivy's eyebrows arching, but it brought a look of relief to Mary Sue's face. "Maybe we could talk at the house. It's such a nice house," she said, looking at Noah.

He glowered.

"No," Ivy said quickly. "I don't live there."

Noah knew that Ivy's objection had as much to do with Lily as it did with her status and the fact that she had never been inside the house. He also knew that Lily and Marta were playing behind the house.

"It's okay, Ivy," he said, and she got his meaning right away. She still didn't look comfortable, but she went.

That was that, except…for the next few days women kept showing up at odd times. Noah considered barring them from the ranch during work hours, but something stopped him. In his mind, he saw Ivy prepared to stand outside until dawn throwing a rope so that she wouldn't be a burden on the roundup. He remembered that her father had tied her to the ranch and…she had lost her child. She was alone in the world, while he still had his little girl. Trying to put himself in her place…losing Lily…he knew the pain would kill him. Nothing would stop it.

But maybe something new, some female friendships would help a little. So, much as he hated this flood of women invading his world, Noah made sure that Ivy's breaks coincided with their visits, and if the visitor stayed a few minutes longer than usual, he didn't say anything.

Ivy, however, protested. "Make sure you yell at me when fifteen minutes is up. I have work. You're paying me," she whispered when she passed him on her way to escort another woman to the house.

"What exactly do they talk about, if you don't mind me asking?"

She shook her head. "Nothing. The weather. The ranch, and...nothing."

But there was an evasive, almost angry look in her eyes. Noah remembered how Mary Sue and the others smiled at him so brilliantly. All of them were, he realized, single. An unpleasant suspicion began to form, one that grew even more the day Sandra Penway came to visit.

"It's good to see you, Noah."

He glanced toward Ivy.

"And Ivy," Sandra said, but she wasn't smiling.

"Sandra." Ivy nodded. She didn't look any happier than Sandra.

"How is Lily? Where is that little cutie? She's just a doll. She's just an angel," Sandra cooed. "Let's go see her together, Noah."

"She's napping."

"Oh." Sandra looked perturbed. "Okay. Will she be up soon? I really want to see her. And, of course, she'll want to see her daddy right away." She held out her hand to Noah as if to lead him to the house. "You and I will just talk until your little girl wakes up."

Suddenly Ivy banged her shovel onto the ground. "I apologize, Sandra, but Mr. Ballenger told me that we need to rebuild the floodgate that washed out after the rain. You know how it is. It's a job that won't wait."

"You and Darrell and Brody can do it," Sandra said.

Okay, that was just wrong, Noah thought. "I don't ask my hands to do things that I won't do," he said. That was true, but there was only one floodgate affected. It wasn't enough work for all four of them.

But Ivy obviously wanted the woman gone. And frankly, so did he. Noah stuck to his guns.

When Sandra had gone, he turned to Ivy. "Thanks."

But he had to know more. "You don't like Sandra. Has she been mean to you?"

Ivy shrugged. "She doesn't like me."

"Why?"

She frowned.

"What?" he asked.

"Basically, I'd say she covets you and she thinks I'm in her way," Ivy confessed.

Yeah, he kind of got the coveting part. "That's pretty disgusting for her to mistreat you because she wants something."

"Yes, but on the other hand, I'm not any better. I lied about the floodgate."

He shook his head. "You kept me from having to play nice guy to someone who isn't all that nice. So we'll make your story true. Brody has plenty of other things he can do."

"I didn't mean to make extra work for you."

But work felt curiously like...*not* work as he and Ivy dived into the messy job of rebuilding the floodgate. They hadn't spoken much during these days when all the women had been visiting, so as he and Ivy worked in concert, he turned to her. "Are you okay with the women of the town now? Tight?" he asked, twisting his fingers together the way she had the day she had lied and told him that.

She shook her head. "They're polite, but I'm not the reason they're here. I'm just the conduit. They want to know about you. And...they ask a lot of questions about you and Lily. I don't like that."

"Because you're uncomfortable talking about her." He hoped he managed not to show how much that bothered him.

"No, it's not that. The things they ask...they want to know what you and Lily do together, what you're like with her, that kind of thing. I remember that day in the store. Some of them, even though they seem entranced by the thought of you peeling off your shirt, were concerned that you weren't raising Lily right. I don't like thinking that they might be spying on you. That's not right. You're a good father."

"How do you know that?" She was never with him when he was with Lily. Her eyes were dark pools of pain when she discussed his daughter, and he knew that a lot of that was because Lily was so close to the age her Bo would have been had he lived.

"I hear it when you talk about her. I *know* it," she said simply, staring into his eyes.

Noah stared right back. Emotion flooded through him, even though he didn't want it to. She was the last woman he could be attracted to, and yet he was.

"You don't know much about me," he argued. "I was a skirt chaser when I was young. Then I met a woman who was spending a summer with her relatives in the next county. She was French, exotic, exciting and different from anyone I'd ever met. I fell hard, and her actions seemed to indicate that she loved me, too, but when summer was over, she left and married a well-connected diplomat with an Ivy League background. She just used me to hold boredom at bay for the summer, and she was amused that I had thought she would settle for a rancher." A bit like the way the women of the town were using Ivy to get to him, Noah realized. He hated that.

"I got in a lot of trouble during the next year. Gillian was a hard lesson to learn, but I thought I'd mastered it. Then I met Pamala. She was funny and quirky and in love with ranching, I thought. So I bit. Two months after giving birth to Lily, she left. She went running off to the next lifestyle she fell in love with—acting—and she left

Lily without a backward glance. So yes, I love my child. She comes before everything. And no, I'm not remarrying or letting anyone separate me from Lily. Now, maybe you know enough about me to say that I'm a good father, because some days I am."

"And the other days?"

"I'm totally petrified, don't have a clue what I'm doing and am scared to death that I'll somehow damage her."

Ivy reached out and touched his cheek. "You haven't damaged her yet. I know damaged. She's not even close. I don't think you could manage it if you tried."

Maybe not, he thought when they had both gone back to work, but he could manage to do something stupid with a woman again, and he was perilously close to doing that with Ivy. Thank goodness he was stopped cold by the thought that Lily would be hurt if he brought a woman into their lives and that woman left.

Because Ivy *was* going to leave. She might think she was through with modeling, but he saw the way she walked and looked. Even her cowgirl clothes had class. He'd found articles on the Internet about her adventures in Paris and Rome. When she was finally through mourning, that life would come calling again. So he couldn't allow himself to be foolish.

A part of him wished he'd stayed firm and not hired her. But mostly he was glad he'd given her the job. While she was here, she made him smile; she made him think. And…she was so alone. At least this job would do one good thing for her by enabling her to pay off the taxes and sell her ranch.

Noah tried to pretend that he wouldn't even notice once she was gone. He didn't succeed. In fact, when Noah woke up in the middle of the night, Ivy was already on his mind. He'd been dreaming about her, and she hadn't been wearing a whole lot in his dream. That couldn't be good.

He sat up with a grunt, flipped on the light and rubbed his eyes as if to rub away the image of Ivy dressed in a short, tight white dress and boots, her blond hair floating around her face as she beckoned to him like a Siren calling him to both ecstasy and doom.

"Stop it, Ballenger," he muttered. "Now." If he was going to think about Ivy, he could at least avoid thinking about her in erotic ways. That would only complicate things.

Besides, now that he was awake and more in control of himself, what he kept remembering from this latest conversation with Ivy was how determinedly nonchalant she had been when she'd told him that the women in town didn't like her, and how haunted she had looked when she'd told him that she knew Lily wasn't damaged because...

He didn't have to finish the thought. Ivy knew about damaged little girls. She'd been a virtual prisoner on her father's ranch and she'd had no female friends. And yet, what he couldn't escape was how polite she'd been to those women even though she suspected their motives. She hadn't called them out. She'd accepted the fact that they had used her as an excuse to get to him. And she'd done it while holding her head high.

Those women were using her, dismissing her, and he knew all too well how it felt to be used and dismissed. He hated the fact that his child would suffer because a woman had decided to use him as a temporary toy, then had walked away. It still burned that he hadn't been able to stop that from happening, that it still messed with his life and his child's life.

Using people...the very subject made him fume, but this situation with Ivy was different from his own. This time he was forewarned. Maybe he could stop it from happening.

Stay out of Ivy's business, Ballenger, he told himself.

But thirty minutes later he was still raging about the fact that he had played a part in this scenario, even if it hadn't been by choice. It was his fault that those women were using Ivy.

"Dammit," he muttered. Ivy had gone through enough. She was more alone than any person on the ranch. He and Lily and Marta had each other. Darrell and Brody had friends. Ivy had no one. She'd grown up in this town having no one. And now when she'd lost so much already…she didn't deserve to be treated as if she didn't even matter. He knew how that could mangle a person's pride, and he wouldn't wish that kind of humiliation on another person.

It made him want to lash out, but Ivy hadn't done that. She'd patiently listened to the women as if she didn't know what they were up to. She'd behaved much better than they had.

Ivy, you could teach those women a thing or two, he thought. And just like that, an idea came to him. A way to turn the tables and give Ivy the upper hand in a very public way, maybe even make up for some of the distress she must have been feeling these past few days. He couldn't go back and rewrite his own history. He had to live with his failures, but maybe he could rewrite this situation. It was a good idea or…maybe not. It was three in the morning. By tomorrow he might decide it was the dumbest idea in the world.

Ivy was up at the house three days later wondering why Marta had asked her to come there. She fidgeted with the pretty braided belt she'd worn. The gold-and-teal scarf at her throat felt a bit too tight. Going to the house still made her uncomfortable, and she hoped she wasn't being called because another woman had shown up. How many single women could there be in a town the size of Tallula? Ivy didn't know, but it sure seemed as if all of them wanted Noah. She braced herself for another woman trying to use her as a front.

But only Marta was there. "I just need a little help with this dishwasher, and Noah says that you're very good at fixing things," Marta said.

In the distance Ivy could hear Lily's whispery little singing. She blinked.

"She's a quiet child," Marta said. "She'll play by herself for hours. You don't have to worry about her."

Ivy knew Marta meant that she didn't have to worry about Lily coming out of her room, but what Ivy suddenly worried about was the other—the fact that Lily played alone for so long that she never met other children.

Like me, Ivy thought, then immediately quashed the thought. It wasn't the same. Noah loved Lily. Ivy's father hadn't loved anything but his ranch. Still, the soft singing tore at Ivy's heart.

She was almost glad when the doorbell rang, but she kept working. Marta called out to her, and, resigned, Ivy came out from under the sink. She washed her hands, then turned to see a plain, pleasant-faced woman looking at her.

"I need help," the woman said. "Noah said you might help me."

O-kay, this is different.

"I don't understand," Ivy said. "What do you need me to do?"

"Make me pretty."

Ivy blinked. "Excuse me?"

"I don't mean beautiful pretty. I just mean different from what I am. And not forever. Just for a night."

"You want to be Cinderella…to…"

Attract Noah, Ivy thought.

"To make my first wedding anniversary special for my husband," the woman said.

Suddenly Ivy couldn't help smiling. She shook her head. "I'm sorry, but could you back up and explain this to me again? What did Noah say to you?"

The woman blushed, and Ivy saw that she wasn't so plain after all. "He didn't exactly say anything to *me,* but my Jimmie was at the feed and seed and Noah was there fielding questions about you. He told the men that when you first started working here, he was afraid that all the women would be starstruck. They had access to a super-model, and he figured that women would be showing up asking advice on fashion or hair or makeup and turning his ranch into a sideshow, but no one did that. And even though women have visited here and you've been polite, not one has asked you to share all the tricks you've learned or asked you to give them a makeover. He couldn't seem to figure it out."

The woman stood there staring at Ivy, her voice a bit breathless. Nervous breathless, Ivy concluded.

She smiled at the woman again even as she wondered why Noah had told that story. He liked his ranch peaceful and quiet and…ranchy, she thought, making up her own word to describe the usually male world of cattle and horses and the men who tamed and traded and watched over them. Surely he knew that at least some of the men would repeat this story to their wives and girlfriends.

"So…you're the first?" Ivy asked with a grin.

"Looks that way. I'm Diane Revner, by the way."

"Nice to meet you, Diane. I'm afraid I don't remember you."

"That's because I'm five years younger than you, so we didn't have any real contact at school. I know why the women haven't asked for your help. They don't want to admit that they don't know everything or that you know more than them. They don't want it to look like they're nobodies and you're somebody. But I'm not proud. Jimmie and I are having a special day. I want to look nice, and not just plain old beauty-salon nice. I want to look special for Jimmie."

"I'll bet he thinks you look special already."

The woman laughed. "He says he does, but I want to do better. Just so you know, I can pay you. If you're working for Noah, you must not be rich anymore."

Some people would have been offended by that statement, but Diane hadn't said it in a rude way, just a commonsense way. That simple fact—Diane treating her like a regular person, not an oddity or outsider—warmed Ivy's heart.

"You know, I think I'd like to do this just for the fun of it," Ivy said. "But I have to tell you, no one has ever asked me to help make them look pretty. I might not be good at it."

Diane looked indignant. "You were a model!"

"That's just luck, good genes and a lot of hard work. Putting makeup on someone is an art, but we'll see what we can do. Can you come back tonight when I'm done for the day?"

"Are you kidding? Ivy Seacrest is going to give me a makeover? Even if I had something planned, I'd cancel!" Diane's smile was infectious, so when the door opened and Noah walked in, Ivy looked up at him, a full-fledged smile on her face.

"Hel-lo," he said, as if he'd never met her before.

"Sorry, Diane, I have to get back to work," Ivy said.

"Not a problem. Thank you so much, Ivy. I'll see you tonight. Bye. Noah, please don't make her work late today. Ivy is going to work her model magic on me."

When she had gone, Ivy looked up at Noah. "Want to tell me why you're promoting me as someone who can fix up the women of the town?"

"Just seemed natural," he said, his gaze steady and noncommittal.

"Natural?"

"You're a model, you've got women trailing out here all the time, and they haven't treated you right. Why not earn a little money off them? It would be justice of a sort. You make them look pretty—they help you pay off your taxes. Finally, someone in the town would be doing something for you."

Now she saw. "Don't feel sorry for me, Noah."

"I don't."

"You do."

He slowly shook his head. "I'm indignant that you haven't been made to feel welcome, but then I didn't exactly welcome you here, either, did I? So maybe I feel a little guilt, too."

She frowned, opening her mouth to speak. He held up one hand. "But don't mistake that for pity. You've handled all this with grace and dignity. You are, as you said, a strong woman. You're also talented, with skills and experience. So no, I don't pity you. And maybe I have my own reasons for doing this, too. I've been used before, as you know. Call it surrogate justice. Besides, there's nothing wrong with you mixing things up a little so that you're the one with the power."

"It sounds as if you have evil intentions. Don't you like the women of the town?"

"I like them fine," he said, which told her nothing. "But I don't like injustice or nonchalant cruelty."

"You're thinking of Lily and how her mother abandoned her."

"I'm thinking of a lot of things. Besides, there's nothing mean about this."

True enough. "So you planted the idea of me giving fashion and makeup advice. You went into town just for that?"

He looked uncomfortable, but then he seemed to shrug off his discomfort and grinned. "No sin in going to town."

No, there wasn't. All her urges to sin were right here, contained in a totally masculine package. Still, she knew that Noah didn't just goof off and go to town on a regular basis. Brody had made that clear to her. And so had her conversation with the women at the store.

"So…did you just take a scattershot approach or did you purposely target Diane?"

"You say that as if I harmed her. I just knew that she's always had a few stars in her eyes. She reads all the fan mags, but mostly I chose her because she's a nice woman. And she doesn't have any interest in me or mine."

Ivy laughed. "In other words, she won't pretend to be visiting me while ogling you."

He crossed his arms over his chest. "If someone says they're here to see you, they darn well should do the right thing and show an interest in you, not show up under false pretenses. I knew Diane would find you fifty times more interesting than me."

Warmth spread through Ivy. He wanted her to get some genuine attention. "Thank you," she said.

"For what? Sounds as if you have an evening of work ahead."

Maybe. The thought of opening a makeup kit made her hands shake. Despite the fact that she had loved modeling and it had been the first time she had ever felt as if she had a place in life...that life was a reminder of another time, one where Bo lived. She couldn't go there. But, Ivy admitted, there *would* be some regret at being the person behind the scenes this time. Maybe even some envy.

That was wrong. Diane was sweet and excited and genuinely friendly. If even a hint of melancholy threatened, Ivy intended to slap it away. Diane deserved better than that.

"Da," a little voice said. Ivy automatically turned toward the doorway, where Lily had crept in unnoticed. The little girl was staring directly at her, all big blue eyes and blond curls. She was clutching a teddy bear, holding him upside down tight against her side, her chubby little hands curled around him. She must have noticed Ivy looking at the bear, because she held him out with a huge smile. "Bunny," she said.

Ivy's heart flipped over. Her throat closed up. There was a pain in her chest, and yet...this was a child, an innocent child. She couldn't run away and risk hurting Lily's feelings. "His name is Bunny?" she asked, with the best smile she could manage.

"Not Bunny. Buh-ny," Lily enunciated with a chuckle. "See? Bunny?" and she held out one hand palm up as if she was sure she had cleared everything up.

"Sorry," Noah said, reaching out and swinging Lily into his arms. "She's quick as lightning, and she sneaks off now and then. Come on, squirt, let's go put Barney to bed."

"Yes. Bunny ti-red," Lily agreed.

"Oh, I see. *Barney,*" Ivy said.

Lily squirmed in her father's arms and turned so that she was facing Ivy. "Yes!" she squealed. "Bye-bye."

"Bye, sweetie."

Noah carried her away, his long legs quickly taking them both out of view.

Ivy dropped to a chair and stared at her hands. She could hear Noah murmuring. She heard the little girl say, "Wuv you, Da. Wuv you, Mar-ta."

Ivy closed her eyes. She concentrated on breathing, on not thinking of Bo. She should get up and leave. But she didn't. When Noah came back, she looked straight up into his eyes. "Don't even consider apologizing. This is your home. It's Lily's home, and she's adorable. I'm the intruder. I'm the one with the problem, and if the tables were turned, I wouldn't want to feel I had to apologize because Bo had acted the way a child acts. She's a sweetheart, Noah. I recognize that. How could I not?"

"But it still hurts to see her."

"It's more than that."

"Tell me."

She hesitated, couldn't find her voice for a minute. She wasn't sure how to say the next thing, so she moved to the door, pulled it open and stepped outside, dragging in great breaths of air.

Noah followed on her heels, shutting the door behind him. "Ivy? Are you okay? Is there anything I can do? *Anything?*"

And that concern jarred the words loose. "I didn't save him. What if I could have prevented it?" Her words came out in a choked whisper.

"You couldn't have. You weren't even driving." So he had obviously looked up the story—or been told about it.

"But I knew Alden liked to gamble, and that included

gambling that he wouldn't get pulled over for speeding, because he liked to drive too fast. He laughed whenever I asked him to slow down. And even though it's been two years, sometimes I still wake up at night and dream that I can live that day over. In my dream I'm not distracted by something else. I'm paying attention and I realize that Alden is in a mood and I keep Bo home. That's all it would have taken. Something that simple. Just that one little decision. If—"

"Don't," he said, grasping her arms in his big hands. "You didn't kill your child, Ivy. You weren't driving," he reiterated. "And your husband wasn't listening to you."

Ivy wanted nothing more than to listen to Noah, to lean into his big body and let him comfort her. He was right. She knew that. And yet he was wrong, too. When Bo had been born, she had promised herself that she would never do anything to hurt him. She had arrogantly believed that she was a much better mother than her own had been. And now she couldn't trust herself. She could never risk having and losing a child again. How could anyone risk having that happen to them again?

Still, the incident today had changed things.

"I don't want you to hide Lily anymore. This is her home, her ranch, her everything. I'll be the one to make the adjustments. If our paths cross…well, I think I handled it okay today. I didn't make her uncomfortable, did I?"

He smiled gently and tucked a finger beneath her chin. "You didn't. She liked you."

"How could you tell?"

"I just can. She talked to you. Usually she has to meet a person several times before her shy wears off."

Ivy smiled a bit at that. "Well, I'd better get back to work. I take it that the dishwasher wasn't really broken. That's why Marta called me in."

"Not broken, I don't think. But I'll check." He turned to go.

"Noah?"

He turned back.

"Thank you."

"What for?"

For not being angry that I have so much trouble being near your little sweetheart of a daughter. But there'd been too much emotion coursing through her this morning already. She'd been on the verge of throwing herself into his arms only moments ago. She needed to lighten things up.

"For going to the feed and seed and telling tales. I like Diane."

"And you don't mind the extra work after hours?"

"It won't be work. And she's only one woman."

"Hmm," he said.

"What does that mean?"

"Maybe…there were a lot of men other than Jimmie at the feed and seed. Some of them have wives."

Ivy smiled. "Well, I doubt that any more women will show up. Diane is unique. But if they do come for makeovers, at least they won't be pretending to talk to me while staring at your muscles. I've been tempted to say something really outrageous just to see if they're actually paying attention."

He grinned at that. "Maybe I should just stare at *your*… um…muscles while talking to the women and see how they like it."

Ivy opened her mouth, then shut it. Walking away, heading she didn't know where, she hoped Noah didn't put words to deeds. If he started giving her another one of those lazy looks that roamed up and down her body, she might make a fool of herself in front of someone who would carry the tale back to every other woman in town. The very thought made her hyperventilate.

It also made her think of Noah's muscles and his strong hands.

She ordered herself to behave. A woman had to be on her toes when she spent her days around animals that could crush a person without even realizing it. "So no more Noah stuff," she ordered.

"Hmm, wonder what she means by that, Brody," Darrell said. Ivy hadn't realized the men were right inside the barn.

"It means I'm in the mood to crack some heads together if you two insist on teasing me and listening in on my mutterings," she said with a wicked grin.

"I don't know what you're talking about," Brody answered, pretending ignorance. "I didn't hear any muttering. Did you say something, Ivy?"

"If I did, I didn't say anything important," she said. That much was true. She couldn't let Noah become important. Her heart couldn't handle any more breaks.

Noah was beginning to wonder what he was doing. A couple of weeks ago he'd been minding his own business, with no thoughts of anything but the ranch and Lily.

Now he was thinking of how warm Ivy's skin had been against his palms through the cotton of her shirt. He was remembering a pair of tortured blue-violet eyes wondering if she'd missed a chance to save her child. He was going to the feed and seed, acting totally out of character and doing really stupid things all because he wanted some justice for her.

Careful, buddy, he told himself. *Don't do anything you'll end up regretting.* He really should just stick to Lily and the ranch. Period. Especially since being a father was such a seat-of-the-pants thing with him. Was he wrong keeping Lily here instead of sending her out into the world...or at least into Tallula? He didn't know. All he knew was that Lily was his. That first step into the world of Tallula and other people would be her first step away from him. Was it wrong to want to stave that off a little longer?

Maybe, but a stubborn part of him didn't want to even be wondering these things. These questions about how he should handle Lily hadn't come from inside *him*. They had come via Ivy, the same woman he'd just been warning himself about.

Warnings about Ivy didn't seem to work. There was something beyond physical beauty that drew him. So when Diane drove up, Noah's antennae went on alert. He was fully aware when Ivy, dressed in a white T-shirt and jeans, walked out to her car to greet her guest. Diane was squealing and practically dancing around with excitement. Ivy looked a bit nervous, but she smiled at Diane.

The women retired to Ivy's cottage, and when they emerged a couple of hours later, Diane looked radiant. Her hair was in a sleek new style, and Ivy had done something to her face that made her look slightly exotic. Polished. Pretty, Noah supposed, although he was already starting to judge pretty by Ivy standards.

"I look so good. Jimmie is going to eat me up," Diane said. Then she shrieked with laughter and gave Ivy a hug before she rushed home to her Jimmie.

Noah started to turn toward the house. He was a bit embarrassed to admit that he'd been spending far more time than necessary making certain all was in order in the barn just so he could ensure everything had turned out all right with Diane and Ivy. He was, after all, responsible for the two women meeting. He would have hated it if things had backfired.

But they seemed good. He smiled to himself with satisfaction and took a few steps toward the house.

"Noah?"

"Ivy?" he answered, turning toward her.

"Thank you once again," she said. "That was fun."

"You did a good job. Jimmie's going to love your handiwork. Not that he'll hesitate for a moment to mess up what you spent two hours fixing."

Ivy laughed. "That's okay. Diane would be disappointed if he didn't get so involved he forgot to be careful. Diane is a sweetie, but I think she might also be a bit of a wild woman."

Noah agreed. "What kind of woman are *you*?" he asked, wondering what he was doing asking something like that... besides running toward the flames.

Ivy studied him. She took two steps toward him. Then she stopped. "I'm a woman who's going to retreat before she does something that might not be smart." Then she turned, walked up the path to her cottage and went inside.

Noah swore beneath his breath—for asking the question and because he knew that he would lie awake half the night wondering what it was Ivy would have done that wouldn't have been smart. And even though he knew she'd been right to retreat, he also wished she hadn't. Because right now he was burning to do all kinds of things with Ivy that they would both regret once morning came.

But when morning came, Noah found that he had a whole different kind of problem.

CHAPTER SIX

WORK STARTED EARLY on a ranch, and Ivy was checking the irrigation lines on an alfalfa field when her cell phone rang.

"We have a situation here. You need to come to the house," Noah said in that deep gravelly voice that—blast it!—made Ivy want to purr.

"A situation?" Immediately all sorts of terrible things started going through her head, though Noah didn't sound panicked. Not that he would. A panicky man wasn't a good rancher. Noah was a good rancher.

"Nothing bad," he said quickly. "God, no. I should have led into that better. Let's just say that Jimmie devoured Diane like a chocolate sundae with extra sprinkles, and now you have a restless group of potential customers waiting for you to transform them into swans."

"I'm working the alfalfa field," she said.

"And I'm grateful. It's what I pay you for. But Ivy, today…I just don't have a way with an eyelash curler or fingernail polish. Seriously, you have to come save me."

She could hear the humor in his voice. "You're enjoying this, aren't you?" she asked.

"I might be thinking that there's some poetic justice in the women who scorned you having to backpedal a little, yes."

"Well, I don't know how I can help them, anyway. Diane was different. I had some free time last night, but sometimes it's late when I finish work. There might not be time to do a full cocoon-to-butterfly transformation. Besides…"

"What?"

"What if even one of them hates it? I might never hear the end of it."

"I hadn't thought of that. So…we'll limit the time to one day. Maybe you'll give a workshop. Charge a fee, give them a few tips, supervise them putting on their own makeup. No one can be upset with you when they'll be the ones doing the grunt work."

Ivy gave a low whistle. "Noah, I have to tell you, if this ranching thing goes bust, you could get some serious work as a talent agent."

He laughed. "Think about the workshop, but in the meantime, come see your adoring public for a few minutes."

He hung up.

Ivy stared at the phone. She wasn't sure she wanted to have a go at it with the women of the town again, but Noah had a point. Her goal was to pay off the taxes. This would help. Besides, by dawdling, she was leaving her boss responsible for entertaining women who were here to see her.

Even the married women would, most likely, be ogling Noah. Hadn't they all been regretting the fact that he rarely came to town? So wouldn't they want an eyeful when they actually got the chance for some time with him?

As Ivy climbed into the truck and drove down the road, she wondered what the women were saying to Noah. Were they quizzing him on his parenting skills, passing judgment?

Ivy gritted her teeth. "Okay, it's absolutely my duty to sidetrack them from that," she told a calf and his mother she was driving past. "A man shouldn't have to explain every move he makes where his family is concerned."

Within minutes she pulled up in front of the ranch house, the pickup truck spitting gravel. Marta let her in, and she moved into the living room, where she could hear voices.

Noah was shepherding Lily around, and all the women seemed to be fixated on the pretty little girl.

But as soon as she moved near, Noah gave his daughter a kiss and signaled Marta, who took Lily off for a nap. Suddenly Ivy was on center stage.

"I understand you want makeup advice?" she said.

"We liked what you did with Diane," Melanie Pressman said. "But I'm only here to scope out possibilities." She looked at Ivy's clothes, her disapproval clear.

"Darn, why didn't I wear my stiletto heels and that sexy red cocktail dress out to the fields?" Ivy said. "In the future, I need to remember to dress better for the cattle."

The rest of the women laughed. Even Melanie laughed just a little.

"Well," Ivy said, thinking about Noah's good idea, "the key to looking good long-term isn't having someone else apply your makeup. It's learning how to make the magic happen yourself. So if any of you are interested, we could have a workshop at my cottage on my day off."

"You can use this house," Noah cut in. "It has more space than the cottage."

Ivy started to protest, but Sandra was faster. "That is *so* generous of you, Noah," she gushed, "but not surprising coming from a man like you."

What did Sandra mean by "a man like you"? Ivy wondered, but of course she knew. It meant that Sandra was trying to suck up to Noah and talk him into her bed.

The thought made Ivy want to step right between Noah and Sandra. Stupid thought. *Don't you dare,* she told herself.

By the time she'd talked herself out of making a fool of herself, the other women had already agreed that Noah's idea was best. The event had been moved to the ranch house.

"Of course, you'll want a fee," Alicia said. "You've got bills to pay, and this kind of expertise would cost a fortune in New York. You just let us know how much."

To her own surprise, Ivy shook her head. "Oh. No. Let's just say—that is, this first one's on me." Had she really said that when Alicia was right and she had just been thinking the same thing a few minutes earlier? Yes, she had, even if it didn't make sense. Maybe it was newcomer's nerves— she'd never taught anyone how to do anything. Or maybe her response had been because a deep-seated part of her didn't feel comfortable accepting money for the kinds of rituals these women had shared as girls. That sharing of hair and makeup and clothing that she'd never shared but which was a part of most girls' teen years.

Stupid. I don't care about that, she told herself. *And this isn't the same at all. They wouldn't have approached you if they hadn't wanted something from you.* But she still didn't name a price.

Instead, she did another dumb thing. She looked directly into Noah's eyes. He was giving her an "are you kidding me?" look and shaking his head. But he was also grinning. Okay, she was pathetic, wasn't she? She needed the money—but she wasn't going to allow herself to regret her decision. She just hoped that her choice didn't partly stem from a desire to prolong her time with Noah. Not accepting money for the workshop meant that she would have to work longer at the ranch to earn her tax money.

Don't let it be that, she thought. She *wanted* to get away from here quickly, didn't she?

"That's very generous of you, Ivy," Alicia said.

"It is," Melanie grumbled, and a few other women also thanked Ivy. Sandra merely gave her a tight smile and a nod.

When the women had gone, Noah walked up to her. "Lady, I think you'd better go back to modeling when you leave here, because business just isn't going to be your forte."

Against her will, she touched her hand to her face. "Not going to happen."

"You're very beautiful, Ivy," he said softly.

She looked up into his eyes. "Modeling requires the illusion of perfection."

"Do you miss it?" he asked.

She wanted to say no. "Sometimes," she confessed. "It was exciting and it gave me validation and a place where I belonged. But I'm fine."

"I think you're wrong about having to be perfect," Noah said. "The world is full of imperfect women and more and more of them are demanding models who look real. Not that I'm an expert, but I read the papers. I see the reports on television."

Ivy couldn't help herself then. She reached up and cupped her palm around his jaw. "You're a good man, Noah."

His eyes turned dark amber at her touch; his lashes drifted down. He turned his head and kissed the palm of her hand, sending heat rippling through her body. "Is that a nice way of telling me I don't know what the hell I'm talking about?"

"It means you're a good man," she repeated noncommittally. She wasn't quite sure what she was even saying. His lips were still just a feather's touch from her skin. She wanted him to kiss her again. But this time she wanted him to kiss her lips. Maybe more.

Her desire must have shown in her eyes, because Noah groaned and broke away. "I may appear to be a good man, but I don't feel like one. What I am at the moment is a man who needs to remember who and what he really is."

"And what's that?"

"A rancher to the bone. This land has been in my family for generations. A Ballenger has always been at the helm. I love this place. I belong to this place. The fact that I'm… distracted right now doesn't change things. We both know that I'm the rancher and you're the model. And Lily is stuck dead in the middle because she's still so innocent that she could decide she likes you, latch on and get hurt when you go."

Ivy sucked in a deep breath. She felt as if she'd been kicked. "I would *never* put a child in a position where she could be hurt."

Noah swore. "You know I didn't mean it that way, or if you didn't…well, there's just another example of how different we are. I rush into things like a bull and say things that come out wrong. I'm a harsh man of the land and you're…not."

Ivy nearly smiled. "No, I'm *not* a 'man of the land.'"

"Don't be cute." He gave her a smoldering look that set her blood to racing.

"Okay. I promise I won't be cute."

"Ivy…" He groaned. "You make me crazy. You have from the start. I didn't want to hire you."

"But you did."

"Yes."

"And now you regret it."

"Yes. No. Yes. Come here." He slipped an arm around her waist and drew her to him. He rested his forehead against hers. Then, without warning, he tugged her closer. His mouth crushed hers. His taste was hot, smoky, masculine…. Ivy thought she might faint from the pleasure as he nibbled at her lips, stroked his big hand down her back and over her hips.

"Kiss me again," she whispered when he released her, but she didn't wait for him to follow her instructions. She cupped his face in both her palms and pressed her lips to his. She licked his lower lip.

He nipped at her. Somehow he got even closer, so close that she could feel every contour of his body, the hard muscled planes, the desire he felt for her. If two bodies could have produced steam, the two of them would have been enveloped in a mist cloud in a matter of seconds.

Instead, a horse whickered in the distance. Lily's and Marta's voices drifted in.

Ivy and Noah separated. "I'm sorry," he said. "One minute I tell you I can't do this and the next minute I'm grabbing you."

"It was a mutual grab," she said, and his lips quirked up in a smile.

"I'm sorry about what I said about Lily, but…this ranch is hers. I'm the current owner, but it's her inheritance. That and the blood that runs through me marries me to this land. And I have a bad habit of linking up with women who anyone with sense could see aren't made for ranching. That's my problem—my fatal flaw, I guess—to keep living this situation over and over. I've made a vow to remember what I am and what I'm not from now on. I can't get involved with anyone temporary ever again. Maybe if it were just me at risk…" He looked at her lips again, his eyes smoldering even more.

"But you have a child," she said, backing farther away. Because he was right.

Noah frowned. "Nothing will ever change the fact that Lily's mother deserted her. And someday I'll have to help her get past the hurt that comes with that. I can't put her in the position of losing someone she loves again. There are lots of things I don't know about parenting, but I know I can't risk her that way."

"That's why you're alone."

"Partly."

She quirked an eyebrow. He shook his head. "I've talked about myself too much today. I'd better get back to work."

And she, Ivy decided, had better get back to sanity. She'd come here to earn money, to leave her past behind and help herself find a future. She'd promised herself that she was through with men, because men had taken everything she valued and loved. Yet she'd turned down money today and she had practically invited Noah to make love with her when she'd never been the type to take intimacy lightly.

She so didn't want to analyze that last fact. So what did she want to do? Or…what *smart* thing did she want to do?

But her brain wouldn't function. She needed to get smart fast. Earn money. Leave. Never come back. It was a mantra she intended to keep repeating. It was her plan.

"From now on I'm sticking to the plan," she muttered

as she headed back to work. But before she could do that, she had to get past the free workshop she was giving.

I wonder where Noah will be while that's going on? she thought. Probably somewhere far, far away. What man would stick around while a bunch of women took over his house to do makeovers?

CHAPTER SEVEN

"Wook, Da," Lily said. "Want wook."

Noah gave his daughter a grim smile. "We can't look, sweetheart. Those women would kick our...behinds if we dared to go in there while they had cream and stuff on their faces and their hair in whatever state women's hair is in just before the magic occurs and they finally get it the way they want it."

Noah was flying blind here. He didn't know what he was talking about, but he remembered too well how Pamala had stomped around if he caught her wearing what she called her beauty mud or when she was touching up her hair color and had some sort of cap on her head with strands of hair sticking out. He was pretty darn sure that Melanie Pressman would put the fear of God into him if he ever caught her like that.

He was equally sure that Ivy would look sexy even with her hair in one of those caps. And if her naked body was dunked in mud...

Whoa, Ballenger, put a stop sign on that thought. This is not the time. Although the truth was that there wasn't a good time for those kinds of thoughts. He was never going to see Ivy dunked in mud. Or naked. Or...

"Da, peez." Lily was looking up at him with those big blue eyes, and his heart nearly broke. He wanted to give his child anything she wanted. And right now she wanted to see the women in the other room.

"Lily," he said, hugging her, "let's go for a walk. Or we'll play on your swings. Okay?"

"'Kay," she said, although he could tell she was just being nice. If she'd been older, she would probably have been sighing with resignation. Man, did he have a way with females or what? Even his own daughter had to take pity on him and cut him some slack.

"Maybe we could look at the horses, too," he said, taking her hand and trying to come up with a better treat than the swings.

She nodded solemnly. It occurred to him that his daughter was pretty serious at times. Probably because she spent so much time with adults. Again, Ivy's suggestion that Lily might like to play with other kids came to him. Was it already that time? Was he just being a selfish jerk keeping her here on the ranch with him all the time?

"Bwooz," Lily said.

Noah shook his head, not understanding.

"Bwooz," Lily repeated. And finally, "Bwoo-ooz." She galloped around, mimicking a horse. Or at least as much as a chubby, tottering two-year-old could manage.

Uh-oh. He was going to have to play "bad dad." Twice in five minutes. "Not Bruiser. He's too mean. Maybe Cornbread."

Lily was on the verge of answering when a shriek and then laughter came from the next room. His daughter turned around and zipped away, heading toward the living room.

"Lily," he called. "Come back here right now."

Lily, in typical two-year-old fashion, interpreted that to mean Run Faster. Before he could react, she had covered ten feet of space and had made it partly down the hall.

Not to the living room—but obviously his own voice had carried to that room. Just as he caught Lily and swung her little body up into his arms, he looked up into a sea of female faces.

For some reason he didn't want to examine, he looked for Ivy's face among them. And when he located her, it was her he spoke to. "I'm sorry. She's just really curious about what's going on."

He expected Ivy to nod or say that's all right and then lead her brood back to their business. Instead, she bit her lip and zeroed in on Lily. "The forbidden is always enticing," she said. "It's okay for her to come in."

He could see that Ivy was nervous, but...oh, there it was. The memory of how her father had kept her from getting to be a regular girl. Dammit. How could he fight that? He couldn't. Especially because she was right. Lily's eyes were glowing with excitement.

"If you're sure she won't bother you," he said.

The women automatically began to exclaim that of course they would love to have Lily join them.

And, of course, he was reluctant to leave her in the company of women she really didn't know. Lily was adventurous to a point. With Marta not there, his child would most likely enjoy herself until she realized that no one she knew was in the room. Plus, these women were busy. Who would keep Lily out of trouble and safe?

No one seemed to think of that, and he didn't know what to do. As a male, his presence would be taboo. He would just have to take Lily elsewhere. Probably crying at being denied a treat.

"I think...maybe a male opinion on our progress would be a welcome addition, too," Ivy suddenly said. "I mean, how can we know if we've achieved our goal of looking our best if we don't have any guys to critique our work?"

The look she gave him was both mischievous and determined. She must know that he was going to be like a ship without a sail offering his opinion on women's beautification techniques, but it was almost as if she'd read his mind regarding Lily. The idea that Ivy could read his thoughts was unnerving. If that were true, she'd know what he was thinking right now was that she looked incredibly beddable in that long white silk robe she was wearing. He wondered what she had on underneath.

Noah tried to blank the thought from his mind. "Always glad to be of service," he said. "Thank you for accommodating Lily, ladies."

Cries of "she's a love, she's adorable, of course we want her here" were uttered, and Noah soon found himself seated in his living room, which had been transformed into something he didn't even recognize. The women had brought folding tables, draped them in white cloth and set up makeup stations. There was a makeshift changing area behind a room divider.

The atmosphere was cheerful. Ivy was fully in charge, too, he noticed. For once, she held the power. "Alicia, be bolder with that lip color. You have the complexion to carry something bright. Melanie, look! You have gorgeous cheekbones, and now we can see them. Here, try this teal dress on. It's your color." And "Sandra, not too much liner. A bit more subtle. There, that's perfect."

The women asked questions. They were almost like children. At one point Melanie even pulled on Ivy's arm to get her attention.

At that, he grinned, and Ivy gave him a look. "No more feed and seed for you," she said. "I must have been insane." Even though she seemed to be enjoying herself.

"What?" Melanie asked.

"Nothing. Just a stupid joke," Ivy said, and Noah noticed

that Sandra gave her an evil glare. He hoped Sandra didn't try to cause trouble for Ivy. She'd had enough heartache in her life already. So he was glad when Ivy smiled. Then she raised one brow and mouthed "Payback." Or at least that's what it looked like.

Indeed, in the next minute Ivy turned to Noah. "What do you think?" she asked, having Melanie try on another outfit. "The black leather jacket or the white one?"

She was laughing at having trapped him. Her eyes glowed. It was the lightest he had seen her since she'd arrived, so of course he had to play along. She'd thought she was going to discombobulate him. *Two can play at that game, Ivy,* he thought.

"Well," he said, rubbing his neck as if he was nervous, "if I was a woman, I'd probably choose the white one. But I'm a man." He gave Ivy a long, long look. "And if I were Bob, I'd choose the black leather. Maybe pair it with a short, tight black leather skirt and some thigh-high boots."

The way he looked at Ivy, he knew that she knew it was her he was imagining in that outfit. Her color got high and she tilted her chin up. He thought he had cowed her.

Then she licked her lips, and heat shot straight through his body.

Quickly she turned to Melanie. "Well, there's a man's opinion, Melanie. What do you say?" she asked, her voice all innocent, just as if she hadn't done that lip-licking thing at all.

"I think that Bob's eyes would drop right out of his head," one woman said with a laugh.

"He'd be blind," another added.

"But he'd be happy," Noah pointed out. Melanie was blushing.

"I couldn't wear that," she said.

"Oh, you could and you shall," Ivy said. "I'm taller than you, but we're close to the same size otherwise. And while I don't have exactly what Noah suggested, I have something close. Might be fun. I think Noah could be right."

"You'd lend your clothes to me?"

"They're just clothes."

But Melanie was looking happy. It occurred to Noah that Melanie had never been the type to look happy. Now she was, all because of Ivy.

At that moment Lily reached for something red. "Oh, no, you don't, stinker," he said.

"Stink," she said, giving him one of her most beatific smiles, the kind that just melted his heart.

"She's such a cutie," Alicia said. "My little Taylor would love her. Ivy...remember what we talked about..."

Noah looked at Ivy, who had apparently lost her sass. She looked decidedly uncomfortable. Still, she gazed right into his eyes.

"The women...that is, we could hear you and Lily talking in the other room, and we were thinking that...a playdate would be nice." Her voice trailed off, but she didn't look down.

"A playdate." He said it as if he'd never heard of the term, though of course he had.

"Yes." Now she was looking bolder. "You know, a chance for Lily to try her wings and mingle with other kids a little. You. Lily. Other parents. Other kids."

"Oh, and you, Ivy. We'd want you there, too. We would never have thought of this if you hadn't brought us here."

She blinked. She was going to balk. Retreat into her hide-from-life shell, but Noah could see what this event had done for her. It had given her something she'd never had here before. Female companionship. Justice.

And hadn't he just been wondering if she hadn't been right about him keeping Lily on too short a rein?

"Name the time and place," he said. "We'll be there. We'll *all* be there."

"I don't think—" Ivy began.

"Part of your job," he said.

"I hired on as a ranch hand."

"I don't remember discussing your duties." They hadn't.

"I just assumed I would only be tending to the ranch."

He looked around at the room full of women attending model-school-for-a-day. It was her day off, but…she got the picture.

"Tell me when and where," she said, too brightly.

"Oh, we'll want you to help plan," Alicia said. "Right, girls?"

And Ivy got roped into the deal, but later after everyone had gone home and Lily was in bed, Ivy knocked on his door. "We need to talk," she said when he let her in. "Someplace private."

No, I need to kiss you, he thought.

"Talk. Right," he said. "Let me make sure that Marta knows I'm leaving, and we'll walk."

When he came back, he held the door open for Ivy and then followed her out, jamming his hands into his pockets. If he couldn't access his hands too easily, he'd be less likely to touch Ivy.

Ivy had changed back into her jeans, and she felt more comfortable. She loved nice clothes and dressing up, but functional clothing centered her. Unfortunately, staring up into Noah's eyes turned everything upside down and obliterated any calm the jeans might have lent her. She walked until they were out of earshot of the house, then turned to him. "I didn't mean to step on your toes with Lily today. I just—"

"Thought you saw a lonely little girl."

Ivy crossed her arms. "It's obvious that she's happy. She adores you, and rightfully so."

"But you think I'm holding her back."

To his surprise, Ivy chuckled. "From what I've seen of Lily, there's no holding her back. She's a little whirlwind. I just thought…it's only one day, Noah. If she doesn't like playing with the other kids, or you don't like how it works out, you can always make it a one-time thing."

"Agreed."

"Noah, she's only two. Okay, almost three, but she's not going to run off and leave you anytime soon."

Bingo. She'd hit a nerve. "I don't like…not being in control."

"I know. Some people are like that."

He swore. "I'm not like your father…or your husband, who wouldn't slow down when you wanted him to."

"I never said you were."

Noah glared at her. "You are an infuriating, pushy woman. You pushed until I hired you. Now you've roped me into this."

"Sounds like I'm the controlling one." Ivy frowned. She shoved her hands into her back pockets. "I *don't* like to be controlling. You can back out. I'll make some excuse for you."

He shook his head. "Dammit Ivy, no. The thing is… you're most likely right. I'm never sure I'm doing the right thing with Lily. She didn't come with an operating manual, and she's so outside the sphere of what I'm used to. She's not a horse or a cow or even a blizzard that snows us in and threatens the ranch. If the other kids have playdates, then Lily is going to have one, too."

Ivy smiled. "And you'll take my place in planning it? After all, you're the father."

He laughed. "Not a chance. I don't have the slightest clue what goes on at a playdate, and I'd just end up making someone mad. Anyway, you're the instigator."

"You just want to see me twist in the wind."

It was tempting to tease her some more. Instead he reached out and brushed his fingertips down her cheek. "I want you to get to know these women. When you leave, I hope you won't hate Tallula so much. Maybe you'll even have some good memories of those of us who are rooted here."

She stared at him. "Why are you doing this for me? The workshop? This? Clearing a path for me with the women?"

"I've experienced injustice. So I want to help you get your just due from the town. Maybe...I don't know. Maybe my reasons are also partly because I can't seem to ignore you, and making you a project is better than the alternative."

"What's the alternative?"

"I think you know the answer to that. But just in case you don't..."

He leaned down and kissed her, no touching other than their lips. Both of them had their hands in their pockets. It shouldn't have been so erotic...but it was. He nibbled at her lower lip.

She opened her mouth slightly, inviting him inside.

He tasted her.

She moaned. The kiss turned hotter, deeper, more frantic, and just when he knew he was going to have to wrap her in his arms, she put her palms on his chest and pushed lightly.

Immediately he stepped away.

"You win," she said. "I can't do this. I have to work for you. Then I have to go."

And he had to let her go. He couldn't risk his heart or Lily's.

"You're right. I'm sorry. It was wrong of me to force myself on you like that."

"Get real, Noah," she said. "I was all but on the verge of asking you to take me to bed. But this is wrong for both of us. I'll keep myself busy with work and organizing this playdate at night. I don't know anything about playdates, either. But I'm going to do my best to make this the best one in the world."

"No pressure, huh?"

"Tons of pressure. I don't want you to have any excuse to tell me I was wrong. Or to have any regrets."

But as she headed back to her cottage, Noah was having all kinds of regrets. He regretted hiring this fiery, beautiful woman who tempted him to do something heartbreaking and tragic again. And he regretted Ivy not asking him to take her to bed.

He was going to remember her saying that for a long, long time.

CHAPTER EIGHT

Ivy LOOKED at her bank account, relieved that she was closer to her goal. Things were getting out of hand, on so many levels. She cursed herself for getting too involved in Noah's kiss. The man just made her want to grab him by his lapels, tear his shirt open and run her hands over his chest, and that had never been her style. She had always been the hide-behind-a-mask type. Sometimes that mask had shown up as a mouthy attitude when she felt threatened, but this frantic desire for physical contact was new. She'd been grateful to Alden for discovering her, and he'd wanted a trophy wife, but there hadn't been this frantic heat.

What's more, what was she doing, agreeing to help with this playdate? True, she had wanted it for both Lily and Noah, because she knew he sometimes felt inadequate as a father and she hated people criticizing him when anyone could see that he would take a bullet for Lily.

Still, the nighttime playdate sessions were getting crazy.

"Um…we've moved the playdate to the community center," she told Noah a few days later. "And…well…it's turned out to be more of a party."

To her surprise, he didn't look upset. He looked amused.

"Losing the battle with the ladies, are you?" he asked.

She wrinkled her nose at him. "I just reminded Alicia that this was kind of an event for you and Lily, and before I knew it, more kids were coming—I think some of them are even coming from two towns over. And someone decided that we needed more playground equipment than we—I mean you—have here, and then things went south. Kind of."

"So...it's just been moved to another venue. That's not such a big deal."

"And there'll be a huge, lavishly decorated cake."

He raised an eyebrow.

"And a pet parade."

"Hmm, that's starting to get more involved."

"With some costumes. Some of the kids—and maybe even the pets—will be in costume." Ivy groaned. "I read about a town that had one of those and—I don't know—the idea just popped out of my mouth and before I knew it..."

He held up one hand. "I get the idea. Is that all?"

She raised her brows. "Isn't that enough?"

"Ivy," he said, coming toward her and tipping her chin up, "Why are you doing all this?"

Okay, it was time to get stubborn. Noah couldn't back out now. "I want this to be spectacular. It's your first. And I want you to...to make memories." She tried not to think of how few memories she had of Bo. "I want you to get the best-dad award. Figuratively speaking."

He shook his head. "I don't need that."

"Yes, you do. I know you want to be the best dad. You already are, in Lily's eyes. I want you to know that no one else will ever be able to question you, either. No one likes to think that their child will hear not so nice whispers about their parents."

Which was probably revealing far too much. "Your father?"

"Not really. He *was* a bad dad, but my mother was just a lost soul. A weak person. Not bad."

He looked grim. "I lie awake nights worrying that I'll mess up and wreck Lily's life. I can't begin to imagine what I'll say when we finally have to have the talk about Pamala and her motivations. I know the temptation for me to lie will be there. I'm hoping I can think of something good to say about her."

"You'll think of something. You chose her for good reasons. And without Pamala, there wouldn't be any Lily."

"That's the best thing about Pamala, at least to me."

"See? There *was* a reason for Pamala."

"But I have to be much more careful from now on. For Lily's sake."

"Good. I'm glad you're putting her first, before your own inclinations."

"That doesn't mean those 'inclinations' aren't very difficult to ignore." The smoldering look he gave her made her weak in the knees.

"I'll try to help. I'll keep my distance."

"From Lily."

"From you. Or at least from all the kissing and touching."

"Ivy?"

"What?"

"I think I'd better go now. All this talk is making it difficult *not* to touch."

She nodded. "You'll be at the playdate tomorrow?"

"Your wish is my command," he teased before leaving.

Ivy stood there, just breathing, trying to control her

reaction to Noah. She knew he'd been trying to make her laugh with his last comment, but...she'd never had a man who even pretended to accede to her wishes. Her heart flipped around like a helpless fish on land. She wanted to run after him, talk to him, be with him.

This was so impossible. She couldn't stay. Her luck with men was...well, Alden had courted her and tried to please her, but after they were married, he had dismissed her needs and wishes. And he had not slowed the car down when she'd begged him to. The conviction that if she had been more proactive, grabbed the wheel, not stayed with him, she might have still had Bo, alive and sweet and beautiful, kicked in again.

But this wasn't about her mistakes with Alden. It was about not making any mistakes with Noah. At least Noah had made it clear from day one that his main commitments in life were to the ranch and Lily. He would devote himself to loving his child, nurturing her property and protecting her from anything that might hurt her, including women on the run. Ivy knew right where she stood with him. He desired her; she desired him right back, but there was no possibility of a future for them. Eventually their paths would lead them in completely different directions.

Needing solace, she went out to the corral and spent some time with Bruiser, another outsider who didn't really quite fit, one who was probably living on borrowed time. She'd been visiting him every day, and the big horse no longer seemed even slightly nervous when she was near. He let her touch him freely while standing perfectly still. He even nuzzled her now and then. If she stayed here, someday she would ride him.

Of course, that wasn't going to happen any more than she was going to spend a night in Noah's arms.

* * *

Noah felt as if he had radar where Ivy was concerned. At the playdate-turned-party, she was all over the place. Organizing food, making sure the crepe paper decorations stayed up and out of the reach of little hands that might stuff pretty much anything into their mouths.

She set the route for the miniature one-lap-around-the-grounds pet parade. She made sure there was music. She made announcements and handled custodial duties when there were spills.

What she didn't do, Noah realized, was interact with the children. The gymnasium of the community center was chock-full of two- and three-year-olds, along with a few older and younger siblings. They tended to move en masse like little lemmings, cute as buttons, following whatever kid had the toy of choice. But Ivy seemed to be able to skirt around them and be busy wherever they weren't.

He knew this had to be kind of a bittersweet hell for her. She clearly appreciated children, but every time she looked at them, she had to be wondering what her child would be like if fate had spared his life. Like it or not, she would imagine what he would look like, how he would move and sound and smell and feel cuddled in her arms. That had to sting like fire, especially when her gaze fell on the little ones, the ones about the age Bo would have been.

Lily was close to that age.

Noah took a deep breath, trying to erase that thought, even though he'd known it all along. It broke his heart that his daughter, his reason for living, should cause Ivy such pain, but there was nothing he could do about it. Lily and Ivy couldn't get close when Ivy would be leaving soon. He knew her ranch and had seen what the taxes were. She'd have enough money to pay them soon.

And then…he didn't know what she would do other

than leave, but judging by the way all the fathers here were looking at her, she was wrong about her modeling career being over. She still had the look men wanted and women wanted to have. Her scars only made her seem more real.

The sound of Alicia's voice calling everyone to attention brought him out of his thoughts.

"Time to settle down," Alicia said. "Ivy's going to read a story. Gather around on the rug."

Ivy looked like a trapped doe. Alicia wrapped her arm around Ivy's waist and led her toward a rocking chair set up at the edge of a blue rug. Noah knew that Alicia didn't have a mean bone in her body, so what was she thinking?

"No," he said, but no one heard him and he didn't want to yell and scare the little ones.

Instead he walked to where Ivy was already in the chair, holding a book. The little ones were eagerly gathering around her, right at her feet.

She looked down at the book as if she didn't see it.

"Ivy, you don't have to," he said, and she looked right into his eyes.

But in the next second, she looked down. A small blond boy was touching her shoe and gazing up at her as if he couldn't wait to hear what she was going to say. Ivy looked as if she couldn't tear her gaze away. Her fingers clenched on the book, folding it nearly in half. If she hadn't been holding something, he was pretty sure that her hands would have been shaking.

Lily, seeing that some other child was taking possession of one of "her" adults, was getting ready to do what she did so well—lift her arms, a request to be placed on Ivy's lap.

The mass of little punkins between him and Lily was

squirming and moving, and he couldn't get to her to stop her without stepping on little fingers and toes. "Lily, darlin'," he called. "Come to Daddy. You can sit on my lap."

His grown-up voice seemed too loud and deep in the midst of the lispy, high-pitched voices of the children, and Ivy looked at him.

Lily was biting her lip, a sure sign that she was going through some heavy-duty overload. It was, after all, her first time in a group of kids, and now he was asking her to make a decision. Her little lips trembled, and she blinked as if she would cry, but to his relief she didn't wail.

"It's okay," Ivy said, her voice slightly strangled and soft. Closing her eyes, she lifted Lily onto her lap. Not cuddling, not holding her close, but holding her nonetheless. Ivy sat motionless, stiff. He could tell that this was torture for her.

Dammit, she didn't have to put herself through this. Lily would survive some disappointment. He started to chart a way through the sea of children, but Ivy was already reading. She managed to make it through with only two stumbles, once when Lily leaned against her and once when the little boy at her feet hugged her leg.

But as soon as she finished, Noah took charge, gathering babies, giving them hugs and turning them over to their parents. By the time he got to Lily and Ivy, the little boy's mother had carried him away.

"You were perfect," Noah said, taking Lily in his arms, and he realized that he might have been speaking to either his child or this pale, fragile-looking yet strong woman.

"Ivy…" he began.

She shook her head. "No problem. Good story."

"One of my favorites." He had no idea what he was

saying, but he could see that she needed things to return to normal, to make small talk.

"So you know it. What's your favorite part?"

He didn't have a clue. He'd been watching her instead of listening to the story. "The ending," he said truthfully, concern in his voice.

His reward was a tiny smile, a hint of color in her cheeks. She was returning to normal. Thank goodness.

Just then, someone called his name. A crowd of women, Sandra among them, descended on him. "So someone finally talked you off that ranch, did they, cowboy?"

"We've been waiting for this day, to get you into town. A man needs more than ranching and men who spit and swear. He needs a little softness."

Okay, what to say to that? "I'm sure you're right," he replied.

It was the right answer. The woman who had made the comment gave him a huge smile. But Ivy looked disgusted, probably thinking that he could be manipulated too easily. For some reason that made him smile.

The women chattered on and pressed close to him, and by the time he had disentangled himself and Lily from the group, Ivy was gone. He caught up with her cleaning up the food table.

"Finished?" she asked sweetly.

"I think I just agreed to about ten dates."

Ivy had to know that he was kidding, and normally she would have tossed out a sassy remark and sparred with him. But this time her eyes didn't throw sparks. She didn't look at him at all. Which told him a lot. What a jerk he was. He knew she'd just gone through hell with all those babies and was probably still not recovered. He knew better than anyone how she used sassiness to hide her pain from the world. So why was he teasing her? Without another thought, he reached out and grasped her, hauling her against his side and supporting her as much as she would allow him to.

"We're leaving, okay?" he told Melanie.

The other woman nodded, a look of concern in her eyes. "Absolutely. Yes. You go, Ivy," Melanie said. "You've been running nonstop. Time for the rest of us to do our part."

Ivy opened her mouth to protest, and Noah had an urge to kiss her quiet. Wouldn't that be just great right here in front of all these women? *Yes,* a part of him answered, but he had the good sense to ignore that thought. Instead, he took her hand, letting the jolt of awareness shoot through him. He savored the softness of her fingers against his and the way his hand fully enclosed hers. "You need a rest," he told Ivy.

"I have work to do back at the ranch."

"Not today. You've already done more than enough for the Ballengers today." He did his best to look stern with her, and she let him. Not like her not to argue, so he was even more concerned. First no teasing, then no arguing? Where was his Ivy?

Not my Ivy, he reminded himself, but his concern didn't subside.

Still, he didn't say anything on the way home. Lily might be only two, but she was good at reading moods. He bided his time, and as soon as they arrived home and he passed a tired Lily to Marta, he turned back to Ivy.

"Come into my study."

"Sounds serious." She smiled and followed him, but her smile lacked its usual punch.

As soon as the door was shut, he turned to her. "I am never putting you in that kind of situation again."

"It was my choice."

"It wasn't your choice. You were caught off guard."

"Alicia meant well. I think she wanted me to feel that I was a part of things."

"I got that. Nevertheless, no more events like that for you. If Lily needs playdates, I'll handle them."

"I did okay."

His laugh was harsh. "You pretty much ran the whole thing. That's a whole lot better than okay. But I saw your pain…."

She held up a hand. "I…I handled it."

"I didn't hire you so that you could be a human sacrifice."

"No. You hired me because you needed a ranch hand and I was so annoying that it was easier to say yes than no."

"And because you're damn good at ranching."

"Partly. But mainly because of the other. Because I was persistent enough."

He finally got where this was going.

"And this persistence…I take it you want to talk more about that."

"I do. Now that we're talking about my persistence and pushy ways, I—something came up today and…"

"And…?"

"For starters, I've invited a few women and children over here next week. Just a small group this time. Not a big deal," she said, plowing right in just the way she had when she'd wheedled him into giving her a job.

"Ivy…" He blew out a breath.

"I know. I'm really irritating when I'm pushy."

"It's not that. It's… I saw how difficult this was for you. Why on earth are you diving in again?"

"I have my reasons."

"Want to share?"

"No. And I don't want to cancel, either. It's already set up. Nothing to do but make sure we have a little food."

Noah shook his head. "You mystify me."

"Sometimes I mystify me, too." She was smiling, trying to tease, but her smile was too bright. This day had taken a toll. On both of them. Only Lily had come through unscathed.

"This event today took up a lot of your off hours, and... Lily had a good time. Thank you."

"You would have made the leap in time, anyway. And I'm pretty sure you won a lot of points with the women in town."

"Ivy, don't try to turn me into a hero. I'm just a man, just a rancher and not a very exciting one at that. When the new wears off me, I don't always show so great."

"Great is in the eye of the beholder," she said.

Noah stared into her eyes. He took a step toward her. Had she just implied that she thought he was great? Was he going to kiss her?

She took a step toward him. And then she stopped. She turned. She practically ran away from him.

CHAPTER NINE

No WAY WAS IVY GOING TO let Noah call off the next playdate because of her, she thought the next day. She might have nearly fainted reading that story, but it wasn't something she was proud of. Those sweet babies had had nothing to do with her loss, and letting them see how she was affected hadn't been an option.

In addition, she'd seen how the women looked at Noah. He'd done his share of helping, carrying the heavy stuff, rounding up stray children. Nobody had been criticizing him for not being an exemplary father. He and Lily had fit right in and...okay, there had even been some single women there as helpers who'd been very interested in Noah. Maybe one of them would one day be Lily's new mother. Maybe someone who had always wanted to be a rancher's wife. Noah's wife.

The knifelike pain that slid through Ivy wasn't surprising—she couldn't deny how attracted she was to him—but it wasn't right, either. She wasn't staying. Ranching could not be her life. She'd spent too long trying to escape it. One day she would wake up and remember that and want to be gone again. She hoped.

Besides, even if Noah was interested in her in a romantic rather than a merely lustful way—which he wasn't— Lily needed more than Ivy could ever give. The little girl deserved so much more than a woman who would look at her and remember another child. Far more than a woman who couldn't hold her or hug her the way every child deserved to be held and hugged.

So we get this next playdate going, she told herself. This time we do it here, in Noah and Lily's territory. They're the hosts. After that, they'll be totally in. Old hands with two playdates and a hosting under their belts. *After that, they won't need me.*

She shook her head. "As if they do now. Don't be silly, Seacrest."

"Are you talking to yourself again, Ivy?" Darrell asked. "I wanted you to help me with Bruiser. He likes you better than he does me, and things get done quicker. But you can't be daydreaming when you mess with that one. Even you have to pay attention to him."

For a moment Ivy thought that the same thing could be said about Noah. She'd passed him on her way out. He was heading off to consult with Brody on an injured cow. But even back in his work persona, all business, all ranch, she had looked at him and remembered how he had tasted every time they'd kissed.

"Ivy?"

"Yeah, I'm good," she said.

"You better be."

That's the truth in more ways than one, she thought. But she concentrated fully and Bruiser was just as much a love to her as he'd ever been. With Darrell he was still jumpy and nervous.

"He doesn't like men except for Noah."

"Men can be a problem," she agreed, causing Darrell to give her a questioning look. But he didn't ask, and she didn't offer. She also didn't retract that thought. She'd been thinking about Noah far too much ever since she'd come here. It was time to concentrate on anything *but* him.

The day of the ranch gathering began as well as Ivy had hoped. The weather cooperated, the house was ready and Lily had had her nap. The mood was a little too heightened, perhaps. Maybe she'd planned a bit too meticulously, and consequently she was high-strung and nervous, Ivy thought, but nerves could be dealt with.

She tried not to think about that little blond boy—Benjamin—showing up.

Instead, she made sure that all the preparations were ready. "Blast off," she said when the first car turned in, headed down the winding drive leading to the ranch.

Noah chuckled. "That monumental?"

"Hey, there may only be a few kids coming, but this is your first hosting job and Lily's first chance to be princess of the children for a day. Try to look appropriately humble and yet dazzled by your guests at the same time," she teased.

To her surprise, Mr. "I'm only a rancher" Noah got right into the spirit of the thing.

When the first guests walked in, Lily's eyes lit up like twin sparklers and she took off in a waddling run to meet them, jabbering so fast that Ivy couldn't understand her. But it was clear to all concerned that she was happy to have guests and was prepared to be a gracious hostess. Noah, following Ivy's instructions and Lily's lead, grinned at his guests and kissed hands.

"Ivy tells me that she's entered me in a contest, and to win I have to make you all decide that this is the best playdate of the year," he teased. "So you just let me know if you're lacking for anything or have special requests, and I'll do my best to make sure you're satisfied."

"You couldn't *not* satisfy, Noah," said Sandra, who had tagged along with Melanie, and Ivy felt a bit less gracious than she had a moment before. Which was wrong.

Ivy decided to switch directions. She had a few baby animals she'd brought out for the children to see and even touch, under supervision.

"When did we get a llama?" Noah asked. The fact that he said "we" made Ivy feel a bit dizzy and disoriented. Not that she would let him know.

"We didn't. We had a calf, of course, and the foal you'll recognize. Possibly even the kittens and puppies, but the others—the lamb, the llama and the goat—are all borrowed from neighbors."

"And what do they get for lending their creatures to us?"

"Well…" she drawled. "Some of them wanted me to get you to take off your shirt and chop wood so they could see your muscles. But I'm pretty sure they'll be happy with a simple thank-you and a smile or two."

"You have a wicked sense of humor, Ivy, but you also made my daughter's eyes glow when she realized that she was going to have four kids at her very own house, so I'll forgive you for your smart mouth."

"Don't forgive me too much. I've lined you up to oversee games."

He raised an eyebrow. "This group understands games?"

She laughed. "No, they probably don't. But they like to play, so we have 'Stand next to the bucket and drop the ball in,' 'jump over the one-inch chalk-line river just for fun' and a simple race where everyone who makes it down the field is a winner. Cam you handle those?"

"Ivy, there are only five of them."

"And only one of you, but…go get 'em, cowboy."

He did, and it was great. The kids had fun, but halfway into the party, Brody came to the door.

"I'm sorry for interrupting," he told Noah, "but that cow is getting worse. I don't know what else to do for her. You've had some veterinary training. It would help if you looked at her. Maybe between the two of us we can figure this thing out. The vet is miles away and in the middle of an operation."

Noah didn't hesitate. He told Ivy that he'd be back soon and he left to tend to his ranch. Because that was what he did. He was a rancher to the bone, she reminded herself. Ranching had to come first.

Ivy was surprised that she wasn't more resentful. It was just the way things were. Not the way she liked them or wanted them, but the way things had to be. Some men were born to be ranchers. And some women were born to keep their distance from ranchers, she reminded herself.

Why was it so difficult to stay away from Noah?

By the time Noah came back, an entire hour had passed. Things should have been winding down. Instead, it looked as if a few more people had shown up. Parents were in small groups. A few children were playing in a corner. But where was Ivy? And where was Lily?

Tension slid through Noah. This didn't look good, and, waving people away, he began a circuit of his house.

As he entered the kitchen, Noah heard Ivy speaking softly. "I know you both want the red car, but look what I have here. I've got a shiny green truck and it has more wheels than the car does. Maybe you can play with the truck…um…Davey, and Lily, you can play with the car and then in ten minutes, we'll switch. Okay? Then you get to play with both of them. All right?"

Uh-oh. Noah knew what was going to happen.

"No…" Davey squealed. Lily quickly caught on and cried no, too, adding a head shake for good measure.

"Truck," Lily declared.

"Oh…um, okay, then Lily, you play with the truck first and then Davey can play with the car first. All right?"

More squeals and protests and even some stamping of little feet. These two had Ivy on the run, and it was clear that she was going to make an effort to appease them again.

Noah drew closer and saw that she was looking nervous and anxious. She glanced up at him. "I—"

"You've been abandoned by the other adults," he said over the squeals of the children. "That's enough, you two. No more screaming or you're both going to get a time out. Right now."

The screaming turned into aggravated whimpering, even though both the kids were wearing full-fledged pouts and looking as if the tears and screams were going to let loose any minute.

"You two little boogers are both tired. You should be taking a nap already, and in a few minutes that's just what's going to happen. But for now, you're both going to sit down with me and I'm going to tell you a story. No more trucks and cars today."

Both kids still looked militant in the cute way only toddlers can manage. They looked as if they wanted to beat him up, but they didn't know how to achieve their goal. And, with no alternative other than an immediate time out, they reluctantly crawled onto his lap and he began to tell them a story of his first horse, Danger, who could do all kinds of funny tricks. At first they stopped whimpering and frowning. Then they began to laugh, but soon, as his voice droned on, both of them gave up the fight to stay awake. Soon he was sitting with two sleeping toddlers in his arms.

Ivy was looking at him as if he'd just worked some sort of unexplainable magic trick. As if he'd hung a few stars in the sky.

"How did you know just what to do?" she asked.

"I didn't. Could have backfired completely, but I've learned a thing or two just by being with Lily. You'll learn, too," he whispered. But they both knew that she wouldn't. She didn't want this.

"I'll go get Davey's mom. And…thank you. I don't like to admit that anything gets the best of me, but I was totally lost." With that, she left.

When everyone was gone a short time later, Noah turned to Ivy. "Quite a gathering. You did well."

She wrinkled her nose. "You missed a few things while you were gone. I bought cute little cups with cows on them, and there were major spills. I should have known those were the wrong kind. I've seen Lily with those little sipper things. The little cows were so cute that I didn't think."

He laughed. "The other adults probably thought they were cute, too. You can't think of everything, Ivy."

"Like the goat eating someone's hair ribbon. I didn't anticipate that."

"Stuff happens when goats are around."

"And that tug of war between Lily and Davey… I was ready to start squealing and stamping my feet, too."

"Been there."

"Yeah. Like I believe that."

"Believe it."

"I would have liked to see you throwing a tantrum."

"I doubt that very much."

"I'll bet you never get mad. I've never seen you get real

mad…except for maybe when I was trying to get you to hire me."

"That wasn't mad. That was frustration. Maybe a little fear."

"Fear? Not a chance."

He laughed. "I didn't want you here. You're too pretty. I knew I would be attracted. And I didn't want that."

"Yes…well…I didn't want to be attracted, either. And I *don't* want to," she added.

His smile was grim, but he was determined to keep it light. "Tantrum? Feel like stamping your feet?"

"No. Yes!" she said, and laughed. "Seriously, though, thank you for helping me. I'm just…not good with little ones."

"You can't give them hard choices at this age. Especially when there are two kids. They're both really tired and both of them want all the attention and all the toys. They need the security of knowing there's a big person they can rely on to keep them on course. There's a certain amount of egocentrism at this age. That doesn't mean they won't show concern if you're hurt. Lily has patted me on the leg, sympathizing when I have a cut and doing her best to make me feel better, but she also often wants what she wants and at that point, at this age, I don't think she's capable of empathizing with Davey or he with her."

When he stopped talking, Ivy was looking at him with that stars-in-the-sky look again. "You *do* win the best-dad award."

"Any dad would be the same."

"No. I don't think so. I mean…how many men would even think about toddlers not being ready to process and empathize with another child when there are toys to be had?"

He shrugged. "When Pamala left, and it was just me

and an infant, I knew I was all that was standing between Lily and…and a lot of bad things," he said, grimacing. He'd almost said the word *death,* that he'd been standing between Lily and death. Just an expression, nothing serious, but with Ivy it *would* be serious.

"You don't have to handle me with kid gloves or censor your speech," she said. "I have to learn to deal with distressing words. Otherwise, I can't function. The truth was that you had to keep Lily safe and alive."

"Pretty much," he said, going along with her plan to speak plainly. "So I did some research. Read theories about child development. I tried to use those to help me make better decisions."

"I'm impressed."

"You should be impressed with yourself. Look what you did today. You entertained a group of children and adults. People had a good time. And…I want to thank you. Lily was in toddler heaven when the kids came through the door. That was all you. I never would have done this if you hadn't pushed."

"You would have done things in your own time. You love Lily too much not to notice how much she likes people. Eventually you would have included kids in that. Especially since you're so good with them. Did you— This is none of my business, but when you married Pamala, how many children did you plan to have?"

He shook his head. "Didn't talk about it. She wasn't into planning, but I always thought I'd have at least a few."

She nodded slowly. "Maybe you still will. Sandra wants you. Real. Bad."

"Not real big into Sandra."

"Why not? She's not so bad. She's pretty."

"I don't know. I never thought about it much. She's

okay." But he knew why he didn't care much for Sandra. Sandra didn't try to hide her dislike of Ivy.

"Sandra probably didn't like your cow cups," he teased. "I'm a cattleman. I liked the cups."

She laughed. "That didn't even make sense, and you know it," she said as she headed for the door.

Yeah, she was right, but then nothing much had made sense since Ivy arrived.

"Do me one favor?" he asked.

"What?" She looked back over her shoulder.

"No more playdates."

Ivy frowned. "Was it that bad?"

"I told you, it was great. I meant it. But you don't need to put yourself through this anymore. I get the idea. I'll take it from here."

She nodded and went out the door. As he looked through the window and watched her walk away, he thought about how alone she was.

That wasn't right, and yet he had more or less just cut her loose. What could he do about that?

Not a thing. These playdates were wonderful for Lily, even good for him, but they were also starting to feel far too much like playing house with Ivy. He was beginning to wonder what it would be like if he could keep her with him. In his house, in his life, in his bed every night.

Didn't he ever learn? If he did any of those things—if she agreed to any of those things—within a year he would be nursing a broken heart, and Lily...Lily would have had yet another woman turning her back on her.

So forget about Ivy, he told himself. But he didn't. Instead, he relived every touch, every kiss. When he woke up in the morning he was as tired and cranky as Lily had been the day before. And he had no patience. He would most likely do stupid things. And lately all his stupid things had centered around Ivy.

CHAPTER TEN

IVY WOKE UP THE NEXT DAY a bit disoriented. Oh, right, yesterday had been that humbling playdate.

Part of the gathering had gone well, but large swaths of it had been characterized by her figuratively hanging by her fingertips over the edge of a cliff. She'd been kicking her legs, not knowing what to do. The cups, the goat and most of all having to have Noah save her from two tiny children. She should have been able to manage, but she had been scared to death that she would do or say the wrong thing and damage their little psyches forever. Years later they'd both be in therapy and remember this moment that they had blacked out of their memories but which had held them back from having a happy life.

Idiot, she said, *Don't be dramatic.* Okay, she was being foolish, but Noah really *had* saved her. Besides, despite her mistakes, she couldn't regret the day. Noah had firmly cemented himself as a good guy. He'd obliterated anyone's questions about his parenting abilities. And then he'd told her he didn't need her help anymore.

That stung a bit. "But it shouldn't," she said to herself. He was the parent. She never would be. He was the one who needed to do all the parenting things.

So they were back to her being just a ranch hand…with

maybe an occasional makeover assignment. Simple. No complications. No kisses.

Good. She could handle that. *Please let me be able to handle this and put some distance between us*, she thought.

So she worked at it. All day.

"You okay?" Noah asked her when he saw her the next day.

"Perfect. Just fine!'" she said, planting the biggest smile she could muster on her face.

Maybe too big a smile. Noah raised a brow. "Ivy…"

"Gotta go," she said. "Work to do. I don't want to get Brody mad because I'm loafing. Have you seen your foreman when he gets mad? He can really ride a person's behind. That's what you pay us for. To work."

Noah snorted. "If it were up to Brody, we'd have a gold-star chart and yours would already be filled. That's how highly he rates your job performance. He thinks that the day starts when you climb up on a ladder and hang the sun in the sky."

"Brody just likes having an extra hand."

Noah gave her a look. "Brody likes having a hand who's a lot easier on the eyes than Darrell or Ed. And he's not wrong about the gold stars, either."

But despite the compliment, he didn't look happy. "Are you sure you're okay?"

Noah's concern for her touched Ivy in a way that frightened her. Because she was growing to care for him far too much. She had to maintain some distance and not fall, not care.

She forced a small, tight nod. "I'm fine. Thank you for the compliment about my work. I appreciate it. I really need to go now."

"I know."

So she went back to work. She pushed herself, did as many chores as she could in as short a period of time as she could. She got sweaty and dirty and tired, but she didn't stop.

When Brody signaled that they should go in for lunch, she shook her head. Noah would be there with Darrell. She didn't want to have to make small talk when her emotions were so turbulent.

"I'm going to go spend some time with Bruiser. He let me put a halter on him the other day."

"You be careful with that big boy. I don't have to tell you how much he could hurt you. One of the dangers of ranching."

Like Noah, she thought.

But Brody's words about ranching's dangers ran screaming through her head just a short time later when she heard Brody shouting, followed by Darrell yelling, "Oh, my God, Noah! Are you all right? No, of course you're not all right. I tipped an ATV half on top of you!"

Ivy's heart went into free fall. Her throat blocked up. She vaulted over the fence and started running full tilt toward the area where the men's voices were coming from.

She couldn't think. Her heartbeat drummed loudly in her ears. When she finally made it to where the men were, Darrell and Brody were both huddled around Noah, who was on the ground. Nearby an ATV was on its side, half in and half out of a ditch.

"Let me see," she said, dropping to her knees beside Noah. He was sitting on the ground, his head down, but when she came up beside him, he looked at her.

"It's nothing. I'm just catching my breath."

"Yes. That's why you're gritting your teeth. And...you're bleeding! Darn it, Noah, don't tell me it's nothing when blood is running down your arm." She started to whip out her phone.

"Done that already," Darrell said.

"Is it just his arm?"

"He might have hit his head a little when I knocked him over. I was doing what anyone knows not to do—looking off to the side when another person is near."

"I'm a little concerned about his ribs," Brody added.

"And maybe his leg," Darrell said. "And…"

"I'm right here," Noah said. "You can ask me how I am."

Ivy stared at him. "As if you'd actually tell us the truth. Your leg—" She reached out to touch his thigh.

"Don't even think about it."

"Does it hurt?"

He gave Brody and Darrell a look that told them to get lost. To Ivy's consternation they did just that.

"You can't just leave an injured man!" she yelled at them.

"Just going to get the truck so we can get him to the house," Brody said.

"Okay. Now about your leg—" she began again.

"It doesn't hurt, but if you start running your hand up my thigh, I'm going to embarrass both of us."

She frowned and shook her head.

"Let me make myself clearer, Ivy. I've got a cut arm, and I'm bleeding, but the rest of my body, though shaken up a bit, is functioning perfectly. And that includes reacting to a beautiful woman's touch."

Ivy knew her face was flaming. "What were you doing when Darrell hit you?"

"Trying to get a calf that had gotten stuck in the mud out of the ditch."

She looked around.

"The collision freed the calf, so no harm done."

Ivy looked down at the blood seeping through Noah's torn sleeve. "No harm done? Right, that's just fruit punch flowing out of your veins. I—darn, I hate ranching. It's dangerous. And don't give me that look. Just…get ready for me to touch you," she said, and she gently grasped his arm and pressed down on the three-inch cut with her palm, trying to stop the bleeding.

"I'm okay, Ivy."

"You've got a lump on your head and you're lucky that it wasn't even worse. I've seen Darrell drive." She frowned at him.

"I know how you feel about ranching and I know I've upset you, but Darrell is a good hand," he said. "Mistakes were made…but occasional injuries go with the job, Ivy. I've had worse."

That wasn't what she wanted to hear or think about. "I know about ranch mishaps. My mother died as a result of a seemingly minor ranch injury that was left untreated, so I know the dangers and that if you live the life, you have to live with the possible consequences. That doesn't mean I have to like the situation."

"I'm sorry about your mother. I didn't know the details. I was away at school at the time."

She frowned. "It was a long time ago, and most people never heard the details. My father locked the world out. But my point about your injury is—"

"I know the point, but this is my life. It will always be my life."

The sound of the truck ended the conversation. Noah insisted he could manage to climb in alone, even though a contrite Darrell wanted to help him. Two hours later Noah was all patched up and resting.

And Ivy was pacing the floor.

Marta came out of Noah's bedroom. "He wants to talk to you, but I warn you, he's mad as fire that the doctor told him to rest for the remainder of the day."

Ivy nodded. She opened the door. Noah lay in bed, a bandage wrapped around his chest, another on his arm. By rights, his masculinity should have been diminished by his injuries. Instead, she felt as if testosterone was being piped into the room. Awareness of Noah as a virile, half-naked man made every cell in her body vibrate.

But she couldn't let that distract her, so she just rushed on with what she had to say. "I wanted to tell you how sorry I am that I insulted your ranch," she said. "I didn't mean it. I was just spitting mad that you got hurt. And I know that Darrell is a good hand, so it was totally inexcusable of me to make those comments."

A slightly amused look made Noah look even more virile. "That was a very polite speech. No attitude at all. And totally unnecessary. I knew why you said what you did, and I like plain speech. I like honesty. A man who's had so much betrayal in his life will always go for the hard-to-take truth over the sweet lie every time. So there's no need to apologize to me. You don't have to love ranching."

"Maybe not, but I could keep my opinions to myself."

He laughed at that, and Ivy could see that it hurt his ribs. She rushed to his side. "Are they broken?"

"Just sore. I might have pulled a muscle."

"Still, it hurts. You might aggravate the pulled muscle. So no more laughing," she ordered, holding out a finger the way one might castigate a child.

"You know, I like your sass, but I'm used to being in charge. Was that an order? Come closer and tell me again." He reached out and took her hand, tugging slightly. She ended up sitting on the side of the bed.

She slowly shook her head. "You're not going to charm my concern out of me."

"Okay. You're allowed to be concerned. I can understand why you would be if your mother died as a result of a ranching accident."

Her mother's death was only a small portion of why Noah's injury had upset her, Ivy realized, but she didn't want to think about those other reasons. That would only make things worse. "Marta said you wanted to speak to me. Somehow I don't think you called me in to demand an apology."

"You're right. I had two reasons. One was so you could see that I was really all right. You didn't seem to believe me when I told you so. If the doctor hadn't ordered me to stay in bed, and Marta hadn't threatened to hide my pants, I would have been up and dressed just to prove to you that I was fit and almost as good as new."

"I knew I liked Marta from the moment I met her."

He smiled. "She's evil."

Ivy laughed, knowing that he adored Marta. "She might be listening," she said, even though they both knew that Marta wasn't the type to listen at keyholes.

"I know," he said, playing along. "That's why I said it. You hear that, Marta? A woman who threatens to hide a man's pants to keep him in bed is evil."

Ivy raised an eyebrow. "Hmm."

He raised both eyebrows. "Well, I might make exceptions for some women," he whispered.

Ivy was surprised to find that her hands were shaking… and she was leaning closer to Noah, as if she might be planning to place those hands right on him. The only thing that saved her from doing just that, from leaning forward and licking his lips, was the thought that someone might open the door and walk in on them. With everyone so concerned about Noah, Brody and Darrell would probably be showing up to check on him soon.

"What was the second reason?" she asked, still staring at his mouth.

He visibly swallowed. He was still holding her hand and he looked down to where he was touching her. He rubbed his thumb over the back of her hand, making her skin sing. She jerked, and Noah released her.

"Alicia called," he said. "Her annual cattleman's ball is going to be this weekend, and the women want to give it a bit of a twist this year. They want to have a mini fashion show to give it some pizzazz. The women want to try out their newfound skills you taught them and walk the runway, have a charity auction and sell their time and company at the ball. It's something they dreamed up yesterday."

"That sounds wonderful. Why did you need to talk to me about it?"

"She wanted to know if I would be willing to give you some time off tomorrow to advise them on what to wear, how to walk the runway and how to pull the whole thing off. I told her that if you agreed to do it, then you were hers tomorrow but only for one day, because I know you want to work and earn your tax money as quickly as possible. Especially after today, I didn't think you'd want to stick around longer than you had to."

Ivy didn't know what to say to that. She knew that, sparks or not, skilled at her job or not, she wasn't what Noah needed in his life. He needed a 100-percent ranch wife, someone who loved ranching through good times and bad. And he needed a mother for Lily. Someone unafraid to be a real mother.

And Lily? There was the rub. She could never know for sure that she wouldn't hurt Lily. She remembered waking at night when Bo was first born, grateful that he was hers and worrying that she might somehow let harm come to him. But eventually she realized that she would never let him get hurt. At least, she had foolishly believed that until…

No, she wasn't going to think about that.

"Ivy?" Noah was still waiting for an answer. "It's your call."

"I'd be happy to advise the women."

"I thought you might. You like to play tough, but you're really very soft." He smiled, but he was starting to look tired.

"Oh, I'm tough, all right. Through and through. That's why I'm ordering you to get some sleep."

"Darn doctor gave me something. Heck, it's not even close to dark."

"For a nice man, you're pretty cranky about going to bed. Come on, lie down."

He looked as if he might argue, but then he started to slide down in the bed. He winced slightly, and Ivy leaned toward him.

"I'm okay," he said.

"Nice try. I'm not buying that story. Now, don't be such a stubborn cowboy. Let me help you."

She reached around him to support him and came right up against his side, her mouth just a whisper away from his jaw. Her hand slid against his bare back.

"I'm too heavy for you. You'll hurt yourself," he said, turning his head, his warm breath lifting a stray curl that had fallen across her face.

Ivy's heart was pounding hard and fast, but she was a woman on a mission. "I'm strong. Just let me…" She lifted the cover slightly, so that he could slide farther down, but he clamped down on her hand.

"I wouldn't advise you doing that. I may be tired, but I'm fully male, and I'm not wearing a thing underneath this blanket. Now, strong or not, let go, darlin'. I won't fight you. I'll rest."

"All right," she whispered. "But be careful. No sudden moves."

"No. Just slow ones." And he turned his head more fully, reached out and cupped her jaw and kissed her. Slowly. Deeply. Then he kissed her again.

"You're a woman of many talents," he said as he let her go and slid beneath the covers. "You can tame brute horses, mend a fence, sell million-dollar clothes to billionaires, organize a playdate and make a man so crazy with just one kiss that he almost forgets what he's supposed to be doing."

Ivy stared down at him. He looked like a big, languorous lion. His hair was disheveled from where she'd brushed up against him, his chest was bare, his eyes...those gorgeous, sexy amber eyes. "You're supposed to be sleeping," she whispered, but she leaned down and kissed him. Or he kissed her. Either way, he tasted her fully. He ran one big palm down her back, over her curves. He groaned.

She jerked back. "Did I hurt you?"

"Not in the way you mean. No. I'm fine."

But she wasn't. She had been halfway to crawling under the cover with him, forgetting that he was hurt, that there were people in the house and that...well, if she didn't start backing away from him soon, she was going to break all over again. And she might break him, too. Or Lily. Neither was acceptable.

"Sleep," she said.

"Yes."

There, she thought, exiting the room. She had backed away. Everything was fine.

But when she came out of the room, there was Lily, looking as if her heart was breaking. "Da?" she said.

Ivy's own heart flipped over. She reached behind her, quietly opened the door and peeked inside. Noah's eyes were closed, his dark lashes drifting down over his cheeks. He'd fought the drug, but the drug was winning.

Silently she closed the door again and, kicking a few bricks out of the emotional wall she'd been building for two years, she bent down to Lily and held out her hand. "Daddy is sleeping. Let's go find Marta. Okay?"

Lily looked up at her with eyes of clearest blue. She nodded slowly, but her chin was trembling. Was it true that children knew when something was wrong with their parents? Ivy didn't know, but Lily was obviously concerned about Noah.

Still, the little girl let Ivy take her hand. Her chubby little fingers were so tiny in Ivy's grasp, so much a reminder of another child's hand that Ivy bit down on her lip. But she managed to smile at Lily.

And Lily smiled back. It was wonderful. It was devastating. Remembering that killer kiss with Noah, and Lily's smile, Ivy swallowed hard.

Run now, she thought. *You're going to get hurt, Ivy.* A rancher is married to his ranch. No child can ever be Bo or bring back Bo.

She kept walking, hand in hand with Lily. She listened to Lily tell her a story about Barney that she didn't understand one word of but pretended that she did.

But that night, she counted her money again. Almost there, and tomorrow was a payday. But tomorrow she'd be in town, away from the ranch. That should have made her feel good. Instead she woke up in the morning think-

ing of Noah and wishing she could stay and make sure
he didn't overdo it. She knew he would push himself too
hard without someone to sass him around.

CHAPTER ELEVEN

NOAH HAD BEEN KICKING himself all week because he knew he'd taken things too far with Ivy that day in his bed. He'd been groggy, but not so tired that his memory had failed him. Just enough so that he hadn't been totally in control of himself. Not that he ever was in control where she was concerned.

Now he was at her cottage waiting for her to come out of her bedroom so he could escort her to the ball. Brody and Darrell had gone separately. Marta was keeping Lily. It would be just him and Ivy—and man, this felt too much like a date. He would have to watch his thoughts…and his mouth…and his hands. *Stop it, Ballenger,* he ordered.

He had just decided that he would be all right when Ivy's bedroom door opened and she walked out.

His thoughts froze. His brain sizzled. She was dressed in a long silver halter gown, the neckline plunging deeply, the honeyed skin of her back exposed. Her hair was loose except for twin silver clips holding it away from her face.

"You look amazing," he said, his words far too tame for what he was feeling. His fingertips itched to touch, to travel over her bare skin. He wanted to nuzzle her neck, to breathe in her scent.

Instead, he held out his arm. "I'd offer you a gold

carriage, Cinderella, but my SUV will have to do tonight."

She smiled. "At least your SUV won't turn into a pumpkin at midnight."

"It has its good points. Nice dress. Nice everything."

She blushed a bit...which only got him hotter. "The gown's a bit much for the cattleman's ball, I'm told, but the women asked me to emcee and they wanted something glamorous and slinky. They've decided that they want to give the auction major attention. Even though it was put together quickly and won't bring much money this year, they thought that if it worked, they could expand it next year and make it an annual event. So I was supposed to vamp it up."

He grinned.

"What?"

"Vamp it up?"

She held out her hands to draw attention to her outfit. "What would you call it?"

"I'd call it a situation where I don't know what the heck I'm talking about. But I like it. A lot," he said, with a chuckle. "So let's go. I can't wait to see the show."

By the time they strolled in, the party was in full swing. People were dancing, and Sandra was cruising the room snapping pictures.

"Let me get a picture of you, Noah," she said.

Immediately Ivy stepped away from his side, and he frowned.

"You have to smile," Ivy told him.

He smiled. Sandra kept taking pictures, making him turn right and left. "Enough," he said. "I'm not the model."

"Neither is she anymore," Sandra said. "No offense intended, Ivy."

Ivy gave her a look. "None taken," she said with her usual cool, but she blinked when Sandra stuck her camera out.

"Take a picture of Noah and me," the woman said. And without even asking, she picked up his arm and draped it around her shoulder.

Ivy quickly took two pictures and returned the camera.

Sandra looked at the screen. "We look good together. Thanks, Noah. Ivy, I think Alicia wants us backstage."

Ivy nodded. She headed for the backstage area.

Noah watched her walking away from him, and it felt like a punch in the gut. A memory of other times, but even more so, a precursor of what was to come. He'd gotten used to having her around, to sparring with her and teasing her and touching her.

But there was just no forgetting that he was merely borrowing her for a while, and one day soon she would leave him forever. She had been temporary from the start and this time, unlike Gillian and Pamala, he had known it. Tonight, seeing her as a glamorous model, there was no denying the truth. She had never been meant to be here, and anyone who tried to hold her would simply be a selfish jerk.

Noah settled down at a table and waited for Ivy to reappear. In her true colors this time.

Ivy took deep breaths. Tonight was certainly testing her composure. Stepping out of her bedroom to meet Noah, wearing glamorous clothes for the first time since her accident, had made her palms sweat. She'd felt naked, exposed, worried that without her cowgirl armor she might not measure up to his expectations.

His reaction had warmed her, excited her, made her

heart ache. For a short time, until they'd run into Sandra, she'd almost felt as if she and Noah were on a date, one where no one else mattered.

Sandra's comments had brought reality crashing down. Now here she was, ready to appear on a stage in something akin to her model persona. People would be looking at her, judging her.

For a moment a touch of the old defiance kicked in, and she was tempted to scrub away the makeup that muted but didn't hide her scars, the reminder of her biggest and most heartbreaking failure.

But this auction was for a good cause—the women were trying to help children and she had agreed to help, too. She needed to be calm, to do this right and not give in to her fears, not let her voice break or her racing heart betray how scared she was.

Ivy swallowed hard. She peered through a small space in the curtains, scanned the room filled with people. Finally she saw Noah sitting there, waiting. He must have seen her face peeking through, because he winked at her.

Her heart warmed. The dread she'd been feeling disappeared. She pulled her shoulders back and waited for her cue.

Anticipation built in Noah as he waited for Ivy to appear. She'd smiled when he winked at her. Now he was eager as a green teenager caught up in his first impossible crush.

He fidgeted as the lights dimmed. Alicia appeared and announced that none other than Ivy Seacrest would be emceeing their runway auction. She explained the rules— whoever bid the most on a model could choose to have either the benefit of the woman's company for the evening or, for the cost of materials above the donation, some of the seamstresses would re-create a replica of the outfit worn by the model. All proceeds would benefit a local charity.

There was laughter in the audience, with various husbands wondering if they would recognize their newly glamorous wives.

But when Ivy came to the podium in her silver dress, the room fell silent. She looked like a princess, with that long blond hair and big blue-violet eyes. She looked like something a cowboy could never hope to have.

"I'm proud to be here for the first annual Cowgirl Runway Rodeo," she said, her voice coming out too soft at first, then growing stronger. "No roping calves or barrel racing tonight, but we hope to raise a lot of money for some needy kids and have some fun, too, so without further ado, let's bring out our models. Ladies…"

There was a round of applause as the women came out for their preview walk. Whistles accompanied smiles as well as some shocked looks. Other than Noah, who had seen the women strut their stuff at his house, no one had been privy to the transformation.

The women hadn't been shy in their choices, either. There was glamour and extreme cowgirl. There was New York chic, business casual and even a touch of naughty.

There were two daises—Ivy provided the runway patter while an auctioneer handled the bidding. The audience and models hammed it up, and everyone had a good time running up the totals. Noah wasn't bidding. He wasn't going to snag some other guy's wife, and knowing what was going down tonight, he'd already sent a generous donation to Alicia. If they didn't reach their goal, he'd donate more after the auction was over. That would be soon. Most of the women were already taken.

Sandra was last, and she came out wearing a long, demure gown in virginal white that played well against her dark hair. Frankly, Noah was surprised she hadn't chosen something racier. Bold had always been Sandra's style.

"Looks almost like a wedding dress," someone said as the bidding started. And bidding was lively between the women who wanted the dress and the single men who wanted dinner with the lady. But Sandra's smile looked strained before it was over. Several times she glanced at Noah, but he knew better than to enter into this. After surviving two relationships built on pretenses, he didn't pretend things he didn't feel.

And then the auction was over. Or so everyone thought.

"Thank you so much, everyone, for being an appreciative and generous audience," Ivy was saying. "I can't think of a single fashion show I've attended or appeared in that I ever enjoyed more."

She had started to back away from the mike when Alicia rushed forward and whispered in Ivy's ear. Ivy shook her head, but Alicia persisted. She touched Ivy's arm. Slowly Ivy nodded.

Alicia took the mike. "Ivy has just agreed to be our last model for the night. She wasn't expecting this. I sprang it on her just now. So I hope you all know what a big favor she's doing us. This is purely to help those children. Thank you, Ivy. And here she is."

Ivy walked to the center of the stage, and someone backstage turned out all the lights except for a spotlight shining on her and a small light for the auctioneer.

She stood there in her regal beauty, scars and all. Cameras flashed. People applauded. For a few seconds she looked as if her knees would buckle. Then she pulled her shoulders back and stood tall.

"Way to represent, Ivy," someone called.

"Let's help some kids who need it," someone else called out.

"Are you ready, Ivy?" the auctioneer asked.

She turned to him and nodded. The crowd grew silent immediately, as if everyone was holding their breath. Noah couldn't help but wonder what Ivy was thinking. She'd clearly been nervous at the beginning, but…now? Was she glad to be back in the spotlight? Scared? He didn't know. He only knew that she looked as if she'd been made for this moment.

Before he knew it, the bidding was hot and heavy, from men and women alike. Women wanted a replica of the dress; the men wanted…

Noah knew just what the men wanted, and he'd be damned if he'd let them have it. The bidding was at $125. He could do better than that. This *was* for a good cause. Besides, he was not going to let some other man spend hours leering at Ivy.

"Five hundred," he said.

A number of people looked at him. Ivy looked at him. "A man has to support his employees," he said.

Someone laughed, then coughed. Some of the richer ranchers even hung in there for a few more rounds, but when the bidding was over, the children's auction was seven hundred dollars richer, and Ivy was his.

Just for the evening, he reminded himself.

She came down the stairs slowly, holding her dress up so that she wouldn't trip. She was wearing silver heels with straps that made him want to see her wearing nothing but those shoes. But the dress looked good on her, too. It shimmered as she walked. A few people slid their chairs to the side to clear a path for her to reach him.

When she arrived, she looked nervous, like a long-legged foal struggling to figure out what to do with itself. Then she smiled.

"Here I am. Do you want the meal or the dress?"

He let his eyes drift over her from head to toe. "The dress is nice, but…"

I want to see you without the dress, he thought. That wasn't right. She'd agreed to this only to help children.

"But I'll take your company for a few hours."

She laughed. "Not much of a treat. You see me all the time."

"But usually I'm just ordering you around and making you fix things, feed things or dig things."

"Yes, you're a harsh boss, Noah." Her laugh…he wanted to do whatever it took to make her laugh again.

"You did a good thing," he said, his voice low. Not a line to make a woman laugh, but it needed to be said.

"I just stood there."

But he'd seen her falter. "It couldn't have been easy."

"I was a little nervous," she conceded. "But once you started bidding, I knew I didn't really have to be the image. I could just be me."

"So…" He stood to pull out her chair. "Tell me about you," he said as if this was a real date. A first date.

"You know about me. I was a skinny girl with braids and an attitude. I had some bad things happen. I got lucky and made it in modeling, some wonderful things and some terrible things happened and now I'm here."

"For now," he said, unable to stop himself.

She tilted her head in acquiescence. "For now. Tell me about you."

"Not much to tell. I was raised on the same ranch I still live on. My family had money and the means to send me to a good college. I married, had a child, divorced and now I'm here."

"For always."

He mimicked her nod of agreement. "For always. But tonight we're both here. You did well. The women are excited, their husbands are excited and the ball has never been this lively."

"Alicia and her crew outdid themselves on the decorations." The entire ceiling was covered in red and silver balloons with royal blue ribbons hanging down. There were red flowers and white candles in gold holders everywhere.

"They did, but I don't want to talk about Alicia's crew. I bought your time, and I know there's more to you than I know. You like horses with attitude. You like flowers. Daisies?"

"How do you know that?"

"I don't, but you had a pot of them on the coffee table in your cottage. And you like...kittens?"

She laughed. "Everyone likes kittens. Even a lot of people who don't like cats like kittens. How did you reach that conclusion?"

"You had a cat calendar on your wall."

"Oh, that. It was all that was left in the store. Not many people buy calendars in the middle of the year."

"So you *don't* like cats?"

She gave him a you're-just-being-silly look. "I like cats. And...I don't know. I like dark chocolate and teddy bears with white fur and the scent of oranges. Now you."

"Whoa, I haven't finished."

"Hey, Noah, do you think you could spare a minute to come play with us?"

He and Ivy both looked toward the area where the band was setting up.

"You're a musician?" she asked. "I didn't know that."

"Can't tonight. I've got a seven-hundred-dollar date," he

told the man, who laughed as Noah turned back to Ivy. "I play…a little, as they say. I had a garage band in college. Not that good."

"You could play now so I could hear."

"Are you trying to get out of our date?"

"It's not a date. It's a business transaction."

"Then let's do business," he whispered. "On the dance floor."

"Oh…I'm not a good dancer."

"I am. It only takes one. I'll do all the heavy lifting and the leading."

"A musician *and* a dancer," she teased. "Who knew these things? You've been hiding your light in the barn, I think, Noah. And I'm not sure all the heavy lifting in the world can make up for my deficiencies on the dance floor." But she allowed him to lead her into the dance.

True to her word, Ivy had two left feet. She blushed every time she stepped on his toe. But she was charmingly game to keep trying.

"You'll get it in time, sweetheart," he said, knowing that there wouldn't be another time.

"You're very good and very understanding," she said as he lifted her into his arms to keep her from falling. "I don't know how you can stand this, and…oh, your arm must be killing you. I didn't even think…"

"Shh," he said, stopping dead at the edge of the dance floor and sliding his hand beneath her hair, the exquisite pleasure of touching her arcing through him. "Ivy, it was only a cut. I'm fine, and I'm totally enjoying this. You're a delight to dance with."

She shook her head, laughing at that as the dance ended. As they waited for the next one to start, the dance floor began to get crowded.

"You're a good sport, Ivy," someone called, which made her blush more.

Sandra and her partner drifted near. She was looking blue fire at Ivy. Then she stopped. "Seven hundred dollars, Noah? For a woman who can hardly even look at your child? Who can't even dance? It's…I'm tired of this. You've been moping around for years because of Pamala, who was almost just like Ivy. And now this. You know she's not right for you. You are *so* totally blind. You don't even know what's good for you." She shoved hard between Ivy and Noah, heading off the dance floor. But her shoe caught on Ivy's dress as she rushed forward. The sound of tearing fabric was loud now that everything had stopped while people turned to see what the commotion was about.

Then Ivy was falling, her leg giving way beneath her as Sandra shoved. She reached out to catch herself just as Noah and several other people rushed forward, but the stampede of moving bodies got between them, making it impossible for him to reach her. The concerned crowd tripped her up more. She hit the floor, her hands stopping part of her fall, but her face catching against a buckle on Melanie's shoe.

Noah felt sick. "Everybody back," he ordered, pushing and sliding to Ivy's side. He dropped to his knees. "Ivy, don't move," he said. "Not until I determine whether you took a hit to the head."

She started to shake her head. "Don't," he ordered.

"I'm…okay," she said. "Really. I'm okay. Just a little shaken. My head didn't even touch the floor. I can get up."

But the ripped hem of her dress was tangled, and he lifted her into his arms.

"Look. Her face," someone whispered.

"Not her face," another person said. "Her fortune. She's a model."

"No. Don't worry. I'm not—" she said, but Noah started to carry her away.

"Hush," he told her. "Don't try to explain. Just rest. I'm getting you home."

She lifted her head and looked at him, then stared at where her cheek had been resting against his chest. "I'm—I bled on your good jacket," she said.

"To hell with the jacket. I'll get a new one. Just..."

"But—"

"Ivy, for once, don't argue. Just let me do this. Just rest."

Noah was so angry that he could barely speak. She had gotten hurt because Sandra was angry at him. At *him*. The anger wouldn't stop swirling.

He gently put Ivy in the SUV and drove home, both of them silent.

"It's my fault she was upset," Ivy said as he lifted her out of the vehicle. "Noah, I can walk."

"Tomorrow. I'll let you walk tomorrow."

"Where are you taking me?"

"To my house. If you wake up in pain, I want to be near, so I can hear you. Don't argue. I need to do this."

So she didn't argue as he carried her to a spare bedroom, sat her on a chair and cleaned her wound. Then and only then did he speak. "What you said before...you're wrong. I'm to blame for not seeing how jealous of you Sandra was becoming. She was upset with *me*. You've had too many irresponsible men cruising through your life, Ivy. I'm sorry."

She reached up, touching her palm to his cheek. "You sound so sad. Did my face get that damaged?" She didn't sound at all alarmed about the possibility that she might have another scar.

"No." He shook his head. "I looked you over pretty good. You were bleeding, but the wound is more of a scrape. In a few days you'll never know you had it. Now, get some rest. There are spare pajamas in the drawer. They're mine, so they'll probably fall off you. And there's a robe in the closet. I'll bring some clothes from the cottage for you to wear tomorrow. Are you going to be okay?"

"I'll be fine. Will you be okay?"

No. He was beginning to think that hiring Ivy was both the best and the worst thing he'd ever done.

"You're an admirable man," she said. "Putting up with my stumbling, giving all that money to Alicia so that I wouldn't have to sit with some strange man."

He stared at her. "You're the only one who would believe that my buying you tonight was a charitable move. I got to dance with the prettiest woman at the ball."

"But it's midnight now," she whispered.

It wasn't. It was only eleven o'clock, if that. But he knew what she meant. Cinderella would be leaving the ranch soon.

"Good night, Ivy. Sweet dreams," he said, kissing her on the forehead.

"Sleep well," she said. But that, Noah knew, would be impossible. Ivy was sleeping in his house. He had never felt so fortunate or so miserable. This was, he knew, as close as he would ever get to her.

CHAPTER TWELVE

IVY HAD TO DO SOMETHING good for Noah. That business with Sandra last night…that had been *her* fault. She'd known that Sandra wanted Noah, and now that Noah was socializing again, women were lining up to take a number and stake their claims.

Ivy winced at the thought of another woman kissing Noah, but that was wrong of her. A wife would be good for him and Lily. She just…couldn't think about that too much.

Still, she wanted to leave him with something good, to do something that would make a difference in his life. But what? What could she do? She'd helped him with the playdate, but he would have managed that on his own eventually. She'd been a good hand, but so were Brody and Darrell and probably Ed with the broken leg.

Wasn't there anything special she could do, some gift she could manage? He'd done so much for her, helping her to fit in here when she'd never fit before. He'd helped her make friends she hadn't even known she missed having. Maybe she'd even be able to use what had happened here to build a new career helping ordinary women feel good about themselves. So yes, Noah had given her a lot. How could she reciprocate?

But when the next day came, she was still wondering.

She was wrestling with a radiator cap on a truck and not doing a great job of it when Bruiser's whinny made her look up and smile. That was Bruiser's "hey, hello there" whinny.

That was when Ivy finally hit on one good and lasting thing she could do for Noah. Bruiser was going to have to go unless someone could tame him. The fact that the horse liked her and tolerated Noah wasn't enough. She wasn't staying, and with a ranch to run and a daughter to raise, Noah didn't have enough time to devote to a horse everyone thought was a lost cause. Maybe she didn't have enough time to complete the task, either, but she was going to try. She'd gotten Bruiser to let her on his back the other day. And while he'd been skittish at first, eventually he'd settled down. Of course, no one knew that. They would have tried to stop her.

Now she would have to be more open about it. She needed to expand Bruiser's horizons.

So Ivy saddled up Bruiser and rode him around the pen. For the next few days she did the same thing. Eventually Noah broached the subject.

"Is this smart?" he asked.

"Maybe not, but I'm hoping you won't order me to stop."

"Like I ordered you to stop pestering me about a job?" he asked with a smile.

"Yes. Kind of like that."

"Just…be careful, Ivy," he warned. "I'm glad you and Bruiser have bonded, but I worry that you'll miss him too much when you're gone."

"I'm willing to risk that," she said. "He needs this." But she didn't let Noah in on her plan.

The next day she called Darrell over. "Have you ever ridden Bruiser?"

He shrugged. "A few times. He threw me on my butt, of course, and he was so scared and spooked that we didn't push it. Noah was going to sell him and it didn't seem as important as the other things we needed to get done at the time."

"But you take care of him more than Brody. Would you be willing to ride him again?"

"What are you up to, Ivy?"

"An experiment. I've seen Bruiser around you. He lets you brush him, but he's nervous and hard to handle. He lets me do those things without any fuss. I want to try something, but...you should first know that I never had any education in how to train a horse. My father was city born and bred. He learned as he went, and the horses he bought weren't the best. They were already trained but past their prime when he got them. So while I know horses and ranching basics, I don't know how to *train* horses. I'm pretty sure that what I want to do is outside the realm of normal."

"What do you propose to do?"

"Have you work with me. We'll brush him together. Then we'll ride him together. He won't buck me off, so maybe he'll get used to you, too, if we do it enough."

"You are one crazy lady, Ivy," Darrell said. "But I'm game. I can't say what Noah will think of this plan, though."

"We'll see, won't we?"

Noah was coming in from checking irrigation lines when he looked up to see Ivy seated on Bruiser with Darrell right behind her, his arms around her waist.

It was the first time he'd seen a man other than himself ride Bruiser without getting thrown. It was also the first time he'd seen another man touching Ivy. Her long blond hair fanned out in the wind, whipping against Darrell's chest and shoulders.

Noah's gut clenched. He admired Bruiser, who was so attached to Ivy that he allowed Darrell to ride him, he admired Ivy for caring enough to try and he admired Darrell, an experienced horseman, for going along with this unconventional tactic. But all that admiration warred with snarling jealousy.

He fought the jealousy and watched them make a triple circuit of the pen. Then Darrell dismounted, opened the gate and remounted. They made a circuit around the barn and pen and returned to where they had begun.

When they had dismounted and seen to Bruiser, Noah walked up to Ivy. "Did helping Darrell make friends with Bruiser just become another ranch duty?"

"I asked Brody's permission. He didn't object."

Noah shook his head and gave her a wry smile. "I think I might have mentioned that Brody has a soft spot where you're concerned."

"I'm grateful for that, but…he's a good horse, Noah."

"I know that, but I don't know if this will work once you're gone. And I really don't want you to get hurt if I have to let him go. Ivy, you know I can't promise I'll be able to keep him."

"I know," she said solemnly. "But I want to try to help you be able to, if it's at all possible. The two of you need each other."

"Ivy…" Noah drawled. "You know Bruiser put up with Darrell mostly because you were up there with him. He's a smart horse. That doesn't mean he'll let Darrell ride him alone."

"We'll see. Soon."

"Don't get your heart broken, Ivy. If it weren't for Lily, I'd promise to keep him, but I can't risk her."

"I don't want you to risk her. But at the very least…
if this doesn't work and you have to sell Bruiser…I want
him to actually be salable." Her voice broke slightly, and
he knew she was worrying about what would become of
the big horse if he was sold.

Noah reached out and brushed a lock of hair back
behind her ear, then slid his palm down her cheek, not
caring if anyone saw. "I'll try my best to keep him, but
just…don't love him too much, Ivy."

She bit her lip and nodded. "I'm trying very hard not
to love him."

For half a second she stared up into his eyes and he
thought maybe they were talking about something else,
something that made his heart feel raw and broken and…
amazingly enough, hopeful. But that was just dumb stuff,
wishful thinking.

This was just about the horse. He wished he could give
her Bruiser, that she could take him with her, so that she
wouldn't be alone. But where she would most likely end
up, there wouldn't be a place for a horse, especially a tem-
peramental one.

And there would definitely be no place for a cowboy in
that world. He needed to start pulling back from wanting
her.

I'll do that. Real soon, he told himself. *Maybe
tomorrow.*

Ivy knew she'd nearly revealed too much of herself when
she'd told Noah that she was trying not to love. No question, she'd segued right from talking about Bruiser into
thoughts of Noah.

But that was crazy talk, so she concentrated on Bruiser
and kept training the horse. In odd moments she and
Darrell worked with him. She even got Brody involved.

With all this attention, Bruiser was getting better, but he still had a long way to go. She hoped she didn't run out of time. For all that Noah had cautioned her, she'd seen him talking to the horse at times, too.

They seemed like two of a kind, both male animals who'd been dealt a bad hand and were learning to get past their pasts. She'd seen Bruiser shy from a man's touch. She'd seen Noah watching Lily when Alicia's daughter lifted her arms and asked for mama. He'd blanched, and Ivy had realized that Lily would never need the word *mama*. And that Noah's position as sole parent left him very alone in some ways.

That upped the ante on training Bruiser and made it more important. She wanted Noah to keep this kindred spirit, she wanted the horse to be saved and, of course, training him kept her busy. No more kissing Noah; no making excuses not to be with Lily.

The truth was that Ivy had finally admitted that she was going to have to learn how to deal with children in a normal fashion. The playdates had only emphasized how difficult and cowardly it would be to spend a lifetime avoiding little ones.

But Lily was a special case. She was Noah's. And she'd already been harmed by one woman who'd left. Ivy could already see, by Lily's fierce possessiveness of Marta and Noah, how strong the child's affections could be. She couldn't risk being the second woman to desert and hurt Lily, and if she didn't make a connection, that could never happen, so the avoidance continued.

Then, a few days after Darrell's first ride, Ivy was inside the barn when she heard Lily's voice close by. "Bo-ooze," she said. "Bo-ooze."

In the distance Marta shrieked, and Ivy dropped what she was holding. She ran out of the barn and stopped dead in her tracks. What she saw made every muscle in her body clench. Lily had wedged herself between the slats in the pen. Her pants looked as if they were caught on the fence, and she was half in and half out of the pen, only a few feet away from Bruiser. One wrong move from the big animal, and—

Ivy couldn't complete the thought. Instead, she moved. Stealthily. Closer to the pen. As she walked, she began speaking softly to both the horse and the child.

"Shh, Bruiser, shh. She can't hurt you. Not at all. See how little she is. You're fine. You're safe.

"And Lily, don't move, love. Please stay very still, very quiet. Like a little mouse. Just. Don't. Move."

"Ive. Bo-ooze," Lily said, and she wiggled, trying to inch forward.

"Lily," Ivy whispered, desperation making her voice tense. She quickly dismissed the possibility of pulling Lily out from behind. The little girl was snagged on something on the inside, and it would take only a second for the horse to hurt her. Instead, Ivy opted to go over the fence to gather up Lily. Once she had her, she could put her body between the little girl and the horse. She was banking on the horse's affection for her to keep him from kicking out at them.

But as Ivy slung her leg over the top of the fence, Lily wriggled again and fell into the pen.

No time to think. Ivy dived, scooped Lily close as she hit the ground and curled the little girl into her body.

Lily had immediately started to cry when she hit the ground and Ivy ran her hands over those little arms and legs, trying to make sure nothing was broken. "Hurt," Lily said as she wailed, and Ivy's heart broke. "Ow, Ive."

Ivy hugged Lily to her, rocking her. "Shh, you're safe, sweetie. You're okay. I promise. I promise. Nothing will hurt you. You're safe. You're safe." Over and over, Ivy repeated the phrase, holding on tightly.

Struggling to her feet while still holding the child close, Ivy moved back to the fence. Lily was still crying, but her wails were turning to snuffles. She had one arm around Ivy's neck in a choke hold, and the other, Ivy realized, was outstretched.

"Ivy? Lily? Lily!" Noah's deep, tense voice echoed, and Ivy realized that even though she was moving away from Bruiser and toward the fence, Lily was reaching toward the horse.

As if he knew the horror going through everyone's minds, Bruiser took a few silent steps backward.

"Give her to me," Noah said, his voice angry.

Immediately Ivy held Lily out to him, but Lily looked at her with such sweet sad eyes. "Bwoo-ooz," she said. As if she knew that her actions had sealed the horse's fate. As if she shared Ivy's love for the horse.

"It's okay, sweetie," Ivy said. But it was not okay. Now that she could get a good look at Lily, she could see a bump forming on Lily's head and the dirt that covered her cheek and extended into the child's hair. She had let Lily get hurt. If she had done the smart thing and grasped Lily from behind, she might have prevented her from falling into the pen.

In the background Ivy could hear Marta wailing about how she had been hanging laundry and hadn't seen Lily slip away from her. Darrell and Brody were whispering about something. And Noah was looking like... Ivy couldn't begin to read the expression in Noah's eyes. When he had first come rushing up, he had looked as if he wanted to swear, but now?

She didn't know. She only knew that her heart hurt

looking at him. "I let her get hurt," she said. "She has a big bump on her head."

"I thought…Ivy, at first I thought…I'm so sorry. I thought you had brought her in there with you."

Pain sliced through Ivy. "You thought I would intentionally risk her?"

"You love that horse."

"For me. For you. Not for a baby."

"I know. I was an idiot. You wouldn't risk her."

"But I did. Not intentionally, but still…I made the wrong choice. If I hadn't been in the process of going over the fence, I could have kept her from hitting the ground."

"She's okay."

"If she'd been higher up or there had been a rock beneath her, she might not be okay. Mistakes were made. *My* mistakes."

"Don't do this to yourself. I was wrong to even think what I thought. Even for a second. Don't beat yourself up, Ivy. I mean it."

But she didn't want to hear that. She had made a bad choice regarding a child. Again. The fact that it had turned out all right this time didn't change the fact that tragedy had been only a breath away. This changed so many things.

He was not going to let this happen to Ivy, Noah decided. Somehow he had to make this right. He cursed himself for that moment of weakness when he had seen Ivy and Lily in the pen, but he couldn't do that over. He could only do his best to quickly repair the damage as best he could.

What the heck did that mean? What could he possibly do? His words hadn't even made a dent in Ivy's disgust with herself. He needed more. A miracle. An army.

"That's exactly what I need. An army." Noah picked up the phone and dialed.

* * *

Ivy was trying to decide what to do. She'd heard via Brody that Lily was all right, but that still didn't negate what had happened. Over and over, she relived that moment when Lily's head had hit the ground and she had been helpless to stop it because she'd gone over the fence.

She didn't even want to think what could have happened had Bruiser charged or kicked before she could get to Lily.

Darkness was falling, but Ivy didn't turn on the lights. She just sat, thinking and trying not to think at the same time. Trying not to remember the panicked, angry look on Noah's face when he'd thought she'd put Lily in danger. He wanted to take it back, but she wasn't going to let him. He'd been right to be angry.

When the sound of a car on gravel was followed by headlights sweeping across the window of the cottage, Ivy blinked. Probably someone turning around, headed for the ranch house.

More tires. More headlights.

She stumbled out of the cottage to see what was happening. But once outside, she found Noah there with Alicia, Melanie and other parents in the town.

"I'm not going to beat around the bush or give you time to think," Noah said. "Everyone here is a parent. Some of them have been parents for years."

"I don't understand. It's night. Why are you all here?"

"Nighttime's a good time for stories," Noah said. "I hope you like stories. Our neighbors have some great ones."

"I—of course," Ivy said, still not comprehending as everyone began opening camp chairs. Someone gave her one while Noah knelt, put a fire starter and a few logs in the outdoor fire pit and lit a match. When the dry kindling caught, he sat down next to Ivy. He reached out and took her hand.

Her pulse began to jump.

"This is the way it goes," Noah said softly. "At one time or another, every parent makes a mistake or two or more. It's impossible not to. You might not know that, because Bo was so very young when you lost him. But I can't bear the thought of you going through life beating yourself up for this afternoon when you were trying so hard to save Lily." He brought her hand to his lips and kissed her fingertips.

No one said a word about that, but Ivy thought she was going to cry…or throw herself into Noah's arms.

"Alicia?" Noah said. "You start."

The woman nodded. "Taylor had been walking for a few months when I looked away for what seemed mere seconds and he totally disappeared," Alicia began. "I nearly screamed myself hoarse. I babbled, I cried. Eventually I found him next to the creek. One more step and he would have fallen in and drowned. I will never forget that day. I still relive it at times, but I'm grateful for the miracle. That's all a parent can be in a case like that."

"Exactly," Bob Pressman agreed. "Our Michael's five, but when he was three, he was in the garden with me, and I was paying more attention to the weeds than to him. He was only seconds from shaking hands with a rattler when I saw him and barely managed to kill the snake. Those few seconds felt like five years. I'm pretty sure my hair started turning gray the very next day."

He smiled at Ivy. "It's life with a child, Ivy. Sometimes it's calm, but sometimes it's one hair-raising incident after another interrupted by moments of pure joy."

She bit her lip. She couldn't speak.

The stories continued, around the circle. Finally Noah

was the only parent left. He kissed Ivy's fingertips one more time before he released her. "I've told you how scared and clueless I was when I discovered that I had to keep Lily alive and safe with no instruction manual to guide me. I stumbled a lot, had some successes and made tons of mistakes. Then, when Lily was about one, I put her in this little umbrella stroller I used now and then, then turned around to get something, but I had forgotten to strap her in. She leaned forward and fell right out. When I picked her up, I don't know who felt worse, her or me. I was convinced I was the very worst parent in the world."

"The worst," Alicia said, pointing to herself, followed by a mix of voices as each person in the circle pointed to themselves.

"You didn't let Lily get hurt, Ivy," Noah said. "You were trying to save her. You put your body between her and Bruiser. She got a bump. It's not the first time she's taken a tumble, and it won't be the last. So forgive yourself. Please. Forgive yourself for everything. Stop torturing yourself for things beyond your control." She knew he was talking about Bo. His voice broke as if *he* was in terrible pain.

With that knowledge, that her misery was hurting others…something in Ivy shattered, and then, indescribably, her heart felt less heavy. Just a very tiny bit, the merest nudge in the right direction.

Noah was still looking at her, his eyes so fierce and earnest that a tear ran down her cheek. She managed to nod, to sob as Noah dragged her close and held her for long minutes, rubbing her back.

Finally she took his proffered handkerchief and blew her nose. "Thank you," she said, sniffling. "You're all so wonderful. Thank you. I can't believe you all came here just to help me feel better about myself."

"You've helped us. It's only right that we should give

back. You're worth it," Alicia said, and everyone murmured their agreement.

As they all began to gather their chairs and shuffle off back to their cars, Noah stayed with Ivy. When the last car had driven away, he looked at her.

"You didn't have to do this," she said.

"I did."

"Okay. Thank you. But I'm all right now. You don't have to stay and comfort me anymore. You can go."

"I don't think I can."

She tilted her head in confusion, and he came up out of the chair. He reached down and pulled her up beside him. "I can't believe how brave you are. You slay me. You make me insane half the time. You make me want you every second of every day. I have to do this. Right now."

He kissed her, his mouth crushing hers.

Ivy clung to him. She looped her arms around his neck, pressed herself to him.

"If I kiss you again, I'm not going to want to stop tonight, Ivy," Noah said, his voice deep and rough. "Send me away if you don't want that."

"I want that," she whispered against his lips. "I want you, Noah. I don't want to send you away."

Together they moved to the cottage. They didn't turn on the lights, but the moon had risen by then, its pale light filtering into the room.

Noah took off his shirt, and Ivy ran her hands over his shadowed muscles. He groaned and pulled her to him, falling onto the bed and lying back with her on top of him. He laced his fingers in her hair and tugged her closer.

She kissed him, fiercely, with everything she had and was.

He reached up and unbuttoned her blouse, peeling it

back from her shoulders. "More," he said, and he undressed her.

"More," she agreed, sliding off his jeans.

In seconds they were back in each other's arms.

"I've wanted you like this from that first day when I sent you away," he said.

"I want to remember you like this long after I'm gone," she answered.

"Remember me...as if I were your first," he said, kissing her, caressing her, making her burn.

"You are my first since...since that day. And anyway, you're only the second..."

"To make love to you."

She shook her head. "Alden didn't believe in making love. He said it was just biology and mechanics."

"In that case, I don't think I would have liked your husband much. And, Ivy, I'm telling you right now, I fully intend to make this about more than biology and mechanics. We're making love. All right?"

Her answer was to cup his face in her hands and kiss him with all her might.

He rolled with her. They touched, they clung, they kissed. Noah was both gentle and fierce.

For this one night, they weren't employer and employee, or rancher and model. As they met each other in the darkness, none of those titles mattered. Noah was heat and blinding light. He took, he gave; he shattered Ivy's world and returned it to her. Different. Better. Whole, she thought, as she drifted into sleep.

She awoke later, cuddled in Noah's arms, his big body wrapped around her. He kissed her neck, the sensitive spot beneath her ear.

"I have to go," he whispered.

"Oh. Of course." That was the way it was done, wasn't it?

"I want to stay here with you all night, but I don't want Darrell and Brody to look at you differently."

She smiled as he kissed her goodbye, but she knew that *she* would look at things differently from now on. She was in love with Noah. He had started her on the road to forgiving herself for losing Bo. And he had blown away every reservation she had and changed the way she looked at her life. Things would never be the same again.

But when morning came, that thought took on a whole new meaning.

CHAPTER THIRTEEN

NOAH HADN'T BEEN WORKING long the next morning when an unfamiliar car pulled into the drive, followed by another and another. The memory of last night's intervention came to him, but there was a difference here. The men and women that piled out of these cars today weren't people he'd ever seen.

"I'm looking for Ivy Seacrest," a man said, holding out a business card indicating that he was a journalist. The woman with him was carrying a camera that must have cost the farm. "Who are you? Do you know where she is? Can we see her now?"

The man was young, but not too young. He was handsome. Too handsome. And he wanted Ivy. Apparently now.

Noah wanted to tell the man that Ivy was his, off-limits, unavailable, but none of that was true. "I'm the owner of this ranch."

"Is Ivy around?" someone else cut in. "I hear she saved a child's life yesterday."

"I hear she did some modeling recently," someone else said.

"Is this her?" another person asked, shoving a photo of Ivy into Noah's hand. It had been taken at the auction, when Ivy was in the silver gown. "Is there any chance that she might be considering a return to modeling?"

"Or maybe movies?" someone demanded.

"Returning to New York?" another person asked.

Noah's heart started to pound. He had a burning desire to find Ivy, scoop her up and hide her. But that wasn't right or fair. "You'll have to ask Ivy those questions," he said. "If you'll wait, I'll find her."

But that proved to be unnecessary. The commotion had attracted the attention of Ivy and Darrell and Brody. Even Marta and Lily had come outside. Lily was scared by the strangers and Noah took her into his arms, holding her while she hid her face against his chest.

Over the top of his daughter's head, he looked at Ivy, walking toward him, her long hair loose and pretty. Her long legs and slender figure showed to advantage in a pair of jeans. She was wearing a pale yellow shirt that complemented her honeyed complexion. She looked, in short, exactly like a model.

"It's her," someone called, and the growing crowd of paparazzi pounced. Mics were shoved in everyone's faces. Questions were rattled off, machine-gun-style. Those close enough to Ivy fired requests at her. Those who couldn't manage to get close settled for Noah and the others.

He wanted to throw them all out, but it wasn't his career that was up for grabs.

"Ivy, you're as beautiful as ever," someone said.

"More beautiful," someone argued.

"I don't think this is the right place for this conversation," Ivy said. "This is a working ranch. People live here."

"And you work here. That's so awesome," someone said. "Ivy, outdoor life looks so delicious on you."

"Did you really save that little girl?" someone asked. "This woman said that you did."

Noah turned to see Sandra standing next to an older man. She was preening, glowing. "I heard about last night," Sandra said to Ivy, "and…well, I had the photos from the dance. I—that night I shoved you…"

She bit her lip. "That wasn't right. I was jealous, even though I knew it wasn't your fault that Noah didn't want me. I'd had my chance. Plus, everyone was so angry with me. I didn't know how to make it right. Then last night I heard about you and Lily and Bruiser, and everything just kind of fell into place. I mean, it *was* kind of a fairy tale— the beautiful model hiding on a ranch doing good deeds while her broken heart mends. So I took my photos and what I'd heard about you saving Lily and I e-mailed the editors of every newspaper I could think of. I have to say, though, that I didn't expect such a big or quick response. I don't really think it was all me. I think some of it was Gerald."

"I didn't save Lily's life— Did you say Gerald?" Ivy's voice cracked a little.

"Yes, Gerald Donich. He said he used to be your agent and he'd been waiting until you were ready. The photo and what I told him about you convinced him that you might be. He's in the car making phone calls." She indicated a black sedan. "I think he might be trying to get a modeling job for you."

Noah felt as if his heart was ripping apart. The crowd of reporters went a bit crazy. They brandished their microphones like weapons, trying to be the one to get Ivy's first response. They jostled everyone else, and Noah had to hug Lily tight. He should take his daughter away from this, but he was worried about Ivy.

Noah half expected her to rush to the car. Instead, she looked at him.

"I'm not answering any questions until you agree to leave my friends alone," she told the reporters. "If you do that, I'll give you a statement when I've had a chance to digest all of this."

Some of the reporters tried to continue asking questions, but Ivy pushed her chin up. She made her way through the throng to Noah's side and gave him an apologetic look. "I'm so sorry."

"It's okay. Just do what you need to do."

She nodded. Then she moved to the car, where her former agent was just emerging. The man wasn't nearly as old as Noah would have liked. In his forties, he had a kinder face than one would expect of someone who worked selling stars.

"I'm so glad to see you, love," the agent told Ivy. "I was beginning to think you might never resurface."

"I don't know that I have."

"You better. I have contracts for you to choose from. Big ones, too."

She shook her head. "Gerald. Look," she said, turning her scarred cheek to him. The cheek that Noah had kissed only last night.

"Ivy. Look," Gerald said, holding out a photo, probably the silver dress one. "You still can make men sweat and women hope. You still can sell clothes and dreams. And look at this. I found this one of you and the horse and the girl on the Internet. Someone must have posted it yesterday, and I passed it on to a few lucky interested parties. Even dirty and with your hair all messed up...or maybe especially because of those things...you look fantastic. This is a look people haven't seen from you before, Ivy. The tough, healthy, tanned cowgirl look. It's going to sell you like you've never been sold before. The public will eat it up. I think we can get commercials, maybe movies, but definitely magazine ads. It's already in the works. What do you say?"

But Noah had had enough. Everything was conspiring against him. Maybe even every*one*. That photo had to have come from either Brody or Darrell's phone.

The end of things with Ivy had come early, and he wasn't ready yet. Maybe he would never be ready. He shook his head. No matter what, he had to pretend he was happy about this. For her sake. That might take some work, some concentration, some swearing at the walls. Still, he needed to get ready and do it.

He carried Lily into the house and proceeded to get ready to lose Ivy.

Ivy wasn't a happy cowgirl. This whole ambush by the press had caught her by surprise, and the hordes of reporters had made it all but impossible for anyone to do their jobs, although Brody and Darrell had tried.

She had heard one reporter bragging that she had managed to get a photo of Noah and Lily with a nice close-up of Lily's face when the little girl had looked up for a second. The woman was planning on looking into Noah's background, including his romantic entanglements. Ivy had no doubt that the story and the photo would be on the Internet within hours.

"I swear, if you don't stop her, Gerald, I'm going to disappear forever," Ivy told him, knowing that Gerald's threats would convince the reporter more than her own would.

But that problem had barely been quashed when Bruiser was recognized as the horse from the supposed baby rescue, and the flashing cameras and unfamiliar people spooked him so terribly that Ivy had to climb into his pen and try to calm him.

That, of course, only led to more photos until finally she simply stood on the fence, stuck two fingers into her mouth and whistled to get everyone's attention.

"I can see that you're all excited, but you're scaring Bruiser and you're going to have to give him some personal space. I wouldn't want to lose any photographers who got too close."

"Is he that dangerous?" one indignant woman asked.

No, Ivy wanted to say, but the truth was that she didn't know what Bruiser was capable of. She leaned over and gave him a hug. "He's a love. Leave him alone. Please."

In the end, it was Gerald who managed to—temporarily—clear the area. "I sent them to town for food," he said, "but you know reporters. They'll be back. They've found a new toy, a story that promises to earn them points with their publishers. So enjoy your quiet time."

"Thank you, Gerald," she said.

"Don't thank me. You know darn well that I want something from you, too." And he outlined all the contacts he'd made, the choices she had. When she left here, she could slip back into her old life if she wanted to. Then he joined a surprisingly docile Sandra back at his car and drove away.

Ivy didn't want to slip back into her old life. She wanted Noah. She loved Noah, she thought, acknowledging the truth. But…she couldn't have him. He might have pulled off that amazing display of friendship with the neighbors last night, but that was because he knew how hard on herself she had been after losing Bo. As for what had come afterward…there had always been lust between her and Noah. Lust could never be enough.

The heartbreaking truth was that she was probably lucky that Sandra had located Gerald. Work would keep her mind off loving Noah. Because she was pretty sure that this was goodbye.

Ivy fought back her tears, and when she went up to the house to apologize for the insanity of the morning, she saw immediately that the man she loved had already moved on.

He smiled at her. "I told you that you were made for modeling and that someday you'd go back."

Ivy wanted to beg him to love her. She wanted to stay. But already another car was pulling up. Marta was looking flustered. All this mess wasn't good for anyone at the ranch. When she'd arrived here, she'd promised Noah that he wouldn't regret hiring her, but he had to be regretting today's chaos and noise and the invasion of his privacy. This ranch was Noah's life. It was his happiness. It was Lily's inheritance.

If I try to stay, Ivy thought, *the ranch and everything about it will never be the same. It will never bring him and Lily peace and the simple joys of being alone with the land. Reporters will be sneaking out here all the time. Changing the fabric of the ranch. If I try to stay, I'll be as selfish as my father and Alden were, putting my needs ahead of Noah's and Lily's. I'll destroy the thing that gives Noah's life meaning. I'll steal his life's work and his home.*

"I...never really thought it would end this way," Ivy said, truthfully. "I never thought I'd be returning to New York."

"It's where you're meant to be," Noah said. "Maybe it's what you were born for. You'll bring joy to a lot of people."

Ask me to stay, she wanted to cry. *Please tell me not to go.*

"When do you think you'll be leaving?" he asked.

Never. Please, never. "It's probably best that I leave quickly. You're not going to get anything done here until I'm gone."

He gazed down into her eyes. "I don't want you to feel unwelcome. I know that I dragged my heels over hiring you, but…you brought something special to all of us."

And he'd brought something special into her life. He'd made her realize that she didn't have to fight the world or save the world. She had value just as she was, and she always had. And while she'd always miss Bo, Noah had helped her begin to forgive herself. She had room for children in her life.

"It's been wonderful working for you, Noah."

"Ivy…" Noah's voice was deep and thick.

"Be happy, Noah. Enjoy being a daddy to Lily."

At the sound of her name, Lily looked up from where she was playing. "Ive," she said softly.

And suddenly it was all too much. Ivy sailed over to Lily, picked her up and hugged her. "Bye, Lily."

"Ive, bye." She waved her little hand, patting Ivy on the arm, and Ivy set her back down and headed for the door.

"Ivy!"

Ivy turned and looked at Noah, who strode toward her and swept her into his arms. He gave her a quick, hard kiss. "If anyone in New York causes you one ounce of trouble, I want you to call me. You have friends here now, Ivy. They'll always have your back."

She gave him a teary smile, then turned and quickly moved back to the cottage. She called Gerald, threw her things into a bag and within thirty minutes, Ballenger Ranch, Noah and Lily had disappeared from her life. Her entire life was packed in a small blue suitcase. Everything she needed was in there. Except for the two things she needed and wanted most of all: Noah, who was the keeper of her heart, and Lily. They belonged to Ballenger Ranch, not to her.

CHAPTER FOURTEEN

NOAH LOOKED UP from his computer to see Alicia standing beside him. "What are you doing?" he asked. He wondered how long she'd been there. Marta must have let her in.

"Was Lily good?" he asked when she didn't answer but only gave him one of those concerned, maternal looks some women were born to be good at. Alicia had brought Lily home from a birthday party.

"Lily is always good. I don't know about you. You look like hell. Brody tells me you're not eating right. He says you're much worse than when Pamala left."

"Brody talks too much."

Alicia shook her head. "You need to call her, Noah. To see how she is."

"I know how she is. I've seen her pictures." He motioned to several magazines lying on the counter.

"That's not the same. Those are posed pictures and they don't tell you anything."

"I had an e-mail. See, she's happy. Look how cheery it is." He pulled out the paper he'd printed it on. "It says, 'I hope you and Lily are wonderful. Say hi to everyone for me. I have a favor to ask. If you decide that you need to get rid of Bruiser, please let me buy him. I'll find a place to board him near me. I don't want him to be alone. Take care and be happy!' That's all. Just this perky little note. She didn't even sign her name."

"It's an e-mail, Noah."

He growled. "I'm giving her the horse."

"Excuse me? I thought you realized that he likes Lily as much as he likes Ivy. He could have hurt her and he didn't. You said something about her being more likely to be stepped on by a cow than by Bruiser."

"I'm giving Ivy the horse," he said stubbornly. "That's what I was doing when you came in. I was looking for stables near her."

"You need to go look in person."

"Alicia, stay out of this. She's happy."

"She's not. In her pictures she doesn't look happy. She looks distant."

"It's just model stuff. A pose."

"I don't mean the ones in the magazines. I mean the ones on the Internet. The real ones. She doesn't look happy to me."

"That's wishful thinking on your part."

"Don't you even care, Noah?"

He looked up at her, and Alicia froze. He knew that his anguish was clear to her. "You love her," she said.

"She doesn't love me back."

"She said that?"

"She never said she did."

"Did you tell her that you loved her? You didn't, did you?"

"That would have been selfish. She had the world waiting for her."

"She'd had the world *ripped away* from her. Maybe she needed to hear that one man cared about that before he just let her leave without so much as an I love you. Oh, why am I even bothering? You're such a pigheaded man.

I will say this one thing, though. Ivy spent a lot of time with women who had been trying to get your attention for years. Pretty women, some of them even beautiful. And you hadn't looked at any of them, because you never intended to marry again. She knew how set you were against remarrying better than anyone."

Noah concentrated on taking deep breaths, on not yelling at Alicia. "She can have her pick of any man she wants, Alicia."

"Yes, as a matter of fact, she can. And if she has no better options, she just might choose someone else while you sit here feeling sorry for yourself."

Then she relented and patted his arm. "Take better care of yourself, Noah. Please." She let herself out the door.

Noah stared at the screen. He was alone—Marta out shopping, Lily sleeping. Just him and his thoughts and his fears. He'd been left behind by women who wanted more than a man like him. And Ivy, who had never wanted to live on a ranch, was the woman that every man coveted.

Gillian had implied that she loved him; Pamala had declared that she loved him; Ivy had never implied or declared her love for him. Given those facts and circumstances, a smart man, especially a rancher, would have to be insane to even try to win her.

I'm already insane, he muttered. He pulled up a photo of Ivy he'd found on the Internet. *Did* she look distant? Was she sad?

Maybe not, but now the seed had been planted. The possibility that she was unhappy was like a hot brand on his emotions. He'd been so sure that she was finally happy now that the world had come knocking on her door, but what if she wasn't? Who was holding her when she was sad? Who was making sure that she didn't get hurt? Who argued with her and teased her? Who made sure that she knew she was special and that what she wanted mattered?

With a muttered curse, Noah clicked to the airline schedules. Insane or not, he was going to the city.

Ivy was midway through a photo shoot, making lists in her mind, trying to think about inconsequential things while trying not to wonder what was going on at the ranch and who Noah was spending his time with. She had purposely not contacted Alicia for fear she would hear that he was dating someone.

A sudden commotion at the door broke into her thoughts and caused the photographer to swear. "Take a break, Ivy," he said as his assistant came in and started whispering frantically to him. "A cowboy? Here?"

Ivy's heart started to pound. They meant a model dressed as a cowboy, right? Not a real cowboy. This was New York. Lots of unusual characters, people who liked to dress up.

"I don't care who you are. I need to see Ivy. I have information about her horse." Noah's deep voice echoed through the studio, and all of Ivy's senses started to slide dizzily. Her emotions went berserk. She was all emotion, all need, no common sense at all. That must have been why she started rushing toward the door.

But she had barely taken three steps when there he was, all six feet of him, broad shouldered, unshaven, his hair tousled, filling up the doorway.

"Ivy" was all he said.

Ivy fought the tears; she fought the urge to run and throw herself into his arms. "Noah," she said. "I can't believe you're here."

"I know. I don't quite fit."

She wanted to laugh at that. She had seen the look on

the photographer's face when Noah had first appeared. Already she could see him envisioning how to fit a cowboy into the spread they were doing.

"You came," she said. "You came." Then she realized how idiotic she sounded. "Why did you come?" Hope filled her soul. She tried to push it aside.

"I...I wanted to find a good place for Bruiser. I wanted him to be with you."

Disappointment and gratitude combined. "But you love him," she whispered. "I—I mean, that's so nice of you."

Now he swore. "I didn't come to be nice."

"I see."

"You don't see, and why should you when I'm doing this all wrong? The truth is that I came because I wanted to see how you were. I needed to know how you were doing, if you were okay. I realized—after someone pretty much kicked me in the head—that I'd left things unfinished and unsaid. In the past...well, I made assumptions with Gillian and Pamala, thinking that they cared when they didn't. I didn't ask. I just assumed. Maybe because I didn't really care enough.

"But with you...Ivy, I don't want to make assumptions. I have to know. I have to ask if you're happy. That's what I came for. You had so many selfish people in your life who didn't even care whether you were happy or what you wanted. I came...for you."

Ivy closed her eyes. She knew she needed to free him from the torture of worrying about her. She had to say that she was all right, so he could be all right, and—

"But even though I was in such a hurry to get to you that I kind of rushed into this trip, I didn't want to just look like some nosy cowboy," he told her. "I wanted to give you some...proof that you and your feelings matter to me one hundred percent, so I remembered that you loved daisies and dark chocolate and teddy bears with white fur."

He turned, and the assistant who had let him in handed him a bouquet of daisies, a box of gourmet chocolates in a gold box and a teddy bear with white fur and a red ribbon around its neck. "I know you can easily buy any of these things for yourself, but the point is…you shouldn't have to. You should know that someone cares enough to make the effort, someone who cares about more than just what your face looks like."

Tears were threatening. Ivy took several steps toward Noah. "You like me for more than my face?"

"Yes, I do, even though it's a beautiful face. And even more beautiful without the makeup." He pulled a handkerchief from his pocket. "Would it be all right if I—?"

"No!" the photographer and makeup artist both yelled.

"Yes," Ivy whispered, tipping her face up as Noah gently wiped the makeup from her lips, from her eyes and her cheeks. Then he kissed her, slowly, sweetly. He made her ache. "Alicia said you looked distant in your photos, but you don't look distant at all to me. You look wonderful."

Ivy smiled. "If I looked distant, it was because I was thinking about you on the ranch. And Lily."

"Well…about the ranch…"

Ivy waited. Something hesitant in Noah's voice made her tense. "Is something wrong at the ranch? Is someone… sick or injured?"

"Shh, no. No, Ivy." He reached out and touched her cheek. "It's just that…I wanted you to be the first to know that I've been thinking about moving. Maybe to New York."

Ivy couldn't stop herself. She took hold of both his hands and stared up at him. "Noah, are you serious? But…I don't understand. Why would you do that?" she whispered. "You need the ranch. You *love* the ranch."

He gazed down into her eyes. "I do. But I love you more, and you're...here."

Tears filled Ivy's eyes. "You said that you wanted me to know that you cared enough to remember the things I liked. I want you to know that I remember what you like, too. You love music and dancing and riding Bruiser like the wind and telling stories to children, and you love Lily's giggles."

He slid his other hand into her hair and cupped her face. "I noticed that you left yourself off that list."

Ivy bit her lip. "That's because I'm afraid to believe."

"Believe," Noah said, folding her into his arms and kissing her. "I'd never lie to you, Ivy. Even if you don't love me, I'm not going to stop loving you. I can't do that."

"And you're going to leave the ranch?"

"I can't be happy there without you, so I'd rather be happy somewhere else with you. If there's a chance you could care, I'd like nothing better than to ask you to live with me and Lily forever, to marry us."

Rising on her toes and looping her arms around his neck, Ivy returned his kiss. "Marry me," she said. "You and Lily please marry me. We'll live on the ranch."

He shook his head. "You hate the ranch."

"No." Ivy shook her head hard. "I don't hate the ranch. I just didn't want to be sacrificed to it."

He swore. "I'd burn it down before I'd hurt you. I—the thing is that I can't sell Lily's birthright, but we don't have to live there."

Ivy smiled up at him. "Unless we want to."

He looked at her, a question in his eyes.

"Loving you and Lily has opened the world to me, not closed it off," she explained. "I love you, Noah. Take me home to the ranch. Marry me and live with me and Lily there forever," she said.

"I don't want you to give up your life's work for mine."

"Hey, I love being a cowgirl! Besides, I'm sure I can find some way to mix modeling and ranching. I'll never feel cheated as long as I have you."

Noah gave her a kiss that took her breath away. "How on earth did I live without you all those years? Thank you, sweetheart."

"For loving life on the ranch?"

"Yes, but mostly for not listening to a hardheaded rancher every time I told you that I wasn't going to hire you. If you'd listened I would have missed loving you so much."

She laughed and stepped back. "You wouldn't even have known what you missed."

"I know. It would have been a tragedy. Instead, it's a love story that's never going to end."

"Finally we agree on something, rancher man," she told him as she launched herself back into his arms.

Ivy stared around her table at all the friends gathered there. "Happy birthday, angel," she told Lily, picking her up from where she'd finished eating her cake and gently wiping her mouth. "I love you."

Lily smiled and hugged Ivy's neck. "Wuv," she whispered in Ivy's ear, and Ivy thought she might break down in happy tears right there.

"Come on, pumpkin, Marta needs some help in the kitchen," Noah said, taking Lily, giving her a kiss and letting Marta take her away.

There was whispering at the end of the table. "What are you all talking about?" Ivy asked.

"This is an absolute perfect picture of you and Noah

and Lily," Alicia said, holding up a magazine cover of the three of them standing next to Bruiser's pen on the day of their wedding. "It may only be a local publication, but you all look so happy."

"That's because Noah finally met his match," Brody teased.

"It's because we *are* happy," Ivy said. "I'm finally right where I belong."

"And I'm with the woman who hangs the sun in the sky every morning," Noah said, looping his arms around her waist.

Everyone looked at where Noah's hands were on her abdomen. "So…have you seen the doctor? Do you know what it's going to be?" Melanie asked.

Noah smiled. "It's going to be loved," he said. "No matter what sex the baby is or what he or she looks like. This baby will be loved and cared for and cherished and protected and…"

Ivy turned in his arms. She placed her fingertips over his lips and then rose and replaced her fingers with her mouth, to the delight of everyone in the room. "I adore you," she said when she came up for air. "And I'm so glad no one else in town hired me. Otherwise I might have missed…you. This." She gazed up at him with joyful tears in her eyes.

Noah was pulling her close to kiss her again when Gerald cleared his throat.

"I'm glad you two are so happy, Ivy. Things are working out grand, but, Ivy, I really want to talk to you some more about that line of outdoor wear you're developing."

Ivy blinked. "Tomorrow, Gerald. In my office. I'll look forward to it. I'm really going to enjoy that project. But right now I'm in the middle of something important."

"What is it? A different project?" His eyes lit up.

Ivy smiled at her agent. "Gerald, I like you, I admire you, I'm grateful to you, but sometimes you miss all the best stuff. The really important stuff. My husband was about to kiss me. This is a happy day for us. Our daughter is three. We're pregnant. We're…"

"Ecstatically happy," Noah offered with a lazy smile.

"Oh, yes," Ivy agreed, smiling back at him. "I'm feeling very…ecstatic right now. So, Gerald, no shop talk today. And Noah, my love?"

"Yes, sweetheart?"

"Please kiss me. Now. Right now. I don't want our baby to be born before I get my kiss."

The rest of their guests sighed, laughed and applauded.

Noah chuckled. "Oh, you are a sassy woman, Ivy Ballenger. I knew you were going to turn my life upside down the moment I met you. I knew you were going to be trouble."

"Is there a problem, Mr. Ballenger?" she asked.

"Not a chance. I love trouble. I love *you*. You're—"

"All yours, Noah," Ivy said.

"All mine," he agreed. "Forever mine. I'll take my kiss now."

"Take two," she said.

So of course he took three. No one minded, least of all Ivy.

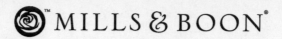

ROMANCE

HISTORICAL

MEDICAL™

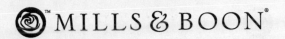

MILLS & BOON

OCTOBER 2010 LARGE PRINT TITLES

ROMANCE

Marriage: To Claim His Twins	Penny Jordan
The Royal Baby Revelation	Sharon Kendrick
Under the Spaniard's Lock and Key	Kim Lawrence
Sweet Surrender with the Millionaire	Helen Brooks
Miracle for the Girl Next Door	Rebecca Winters
Mother of the Bride	Caroline Anderson
What's A Housekeeper To Do?	Jennie Adams
Tipping the Waitress with Diamonds	Nina Harrington

HISTORICAL

Practical Widow to Passionate Mistress	Louise Allen
Major Westhaven's Unwilling Ward	Emily Bascom
Her Banished Lord	Carol Townend

MEDICAL™

The Nurse's Brooding Boss	Laura Iding
Emergency Doctor and Cinderella	Melanie Milburne
City Surgeon, Small Town Miracle	Marion Lennox
Bachelor Dad, Girl Next Door	Sharon Archer
A Baby for the Flying Doctor	Lucy Clark
Nurse, Nanny...Bride!	Alison Roberts

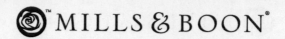

MILLS & BOON

NOVEMBER 2010 HARDBACK TITLES

ROMANCE

The Dutiful Wife	Penny Jordan
His Christmas Virgin	Carole Mortimer
Public Marriage, Private Secrets	Helen Bianchin
Forbidden or For Bedding?	Julia James
The Twelve Nights of Christmas	Sarah Morgan
In Christofides' Keeping	Abby Green
The Italian's Blushing Gardener	Christina Hollis
The Socialite and the Cattle King	Lindsay Armstrong
Tabloid Affair, Secretly Pregnant!	Mira Lyn Kelly
Maharaja's Mistress	Susan Stephens
Christmas with her Boss	Marion Lennox
Firefighter's Doorstep Baby	Barbara McMahon
Daddy by Christmas	Patricia Thayer
Christmas Magic on the Mountain	Melissa McClone
A FAIRYTALE CHRISTMAS	Susan Meier & Barbara Wallace
The Soldier's Untamed Heart	Nikki Logan
Dr Zinetti's Snowkissed Bride	Sarah Morgan
The Christmas Baby Bump	Lynne Marshall

HISTORICAL

Courting Miss Vallois	Gail Whitiker
Reprobate Lord, Runaway Lady	Isabelle Goddard
The Bride Wore Scandal	Helen Dickson

MEDICAL™

Christmas in Bluebell Cove	Abigail Gordon
The Village Nurse's Happy-Ever-After	Abigail Gordon
The Most Magical Gift of All	Fiona Lowe
Christmas Miracle: A Family	Dianne Drake

ROMANCE

A Night, A Secret...A Child	Miranda Lee
His Untamed Innocent	Sara Craven
The Greek's Pregnant Lover	Lucy Monroe
The Mélendez Forgotten Marriage	Melanie Milburne
Australia's Most Eligible Bachelor	Margaret Way
The Bridesmaid's Secret	Fiona Harper
Cinderella: Hired by the Prince	Marion Lennox
The Sheikh's Destiny	Melissa James

HISTORICAL

The Earl's Runaway Bride	Sarah Mallory
The Wayward Debutante	Sarah Elliott
The Laird's Captive Wife	Joanna Fulford

MEDICAL™

The Surgeon's Miracle	Caroline Anderson
Dr Di Angelo's Baby Bombshell	Janice Lynn
Newborn Needs a Dad	Dianne Drake
His Motherless Little Twins	Dianne Drake
Wedding Bells for the Village Nurse	Abigail Gordon
Her Long-Lost Husband	Josie Metcalfe